Susan Stephens was a professional singer before meeting her husband on the tiny Mediterranean island of Malta. In true Modern™ Romance style they met on Monday, became engaged on Friday, and were married three months after that. Almost thirty years and three children later, they are still in love. (Susan does not advise her children to return home one day with a similar story, as she may not take the news with the same fortitude as her own mother!)

Susan had written several non-fiction books when fate took a hand. At a charity costume ball there was an after-dinner auction. One of the lots, 'Spend a Day with an Author', had been donated by Mills & Boon® author Penny Jordan. Susan's husband bought this lot, and Penny was to become not just a great friend but a wonderful mentor, who encouraged Susan to write romance.

Susan loves her family, her pets, her friends, and her writing. She enjoys entertaining, travel, and going to the theatre. She reads, cooks, and plays the piano to relax, and can occasionally be found throwing herself off mountains on a pair of skis or galloping through the countryside. Visit Susan's website: www.susanstephens.net—she loves to hear from her readers all around the world!

CHAPTER ONE

MAGENTA yelped with alarm as a scuffed biker's boot slammed onto the ground within inches of her feet. 'What the hell do you think you're doing?' she exploded, frantically clutching the armful of documents threatening to spill from her arms.

Taking off his helmet, the man shook out a mop of inky-black hair. He was exactly the type of man you didn't want to see when you'd had the day from hell and looked like you'd been dragged through a hedge backwards: gorgeous, cool, and commanding. He had 'danger' flashing round him like neon lights.

'Well?' Magenta demanded furiously. 'Do you always ride a motorcycle like a maniac?'

'Always,' he drawled.

'I should report you.'

Eyes the colour of a storm-tossed ocean laughed back at her.

And she would report him, Magenta determined, just as soon as she sorted out the flat on her car, along with a million and one other things.

Such as her father deciding to retire and sell his shares to some stranger without a word to her. Such as saving her colleagues' jobs from this unknown predator. Such as wanting to get back to her team and their fast-moving, retro ad campaign set in Magenta's favourite era, the sixties.

'Do you mind?' she said, trying to skirt around the man's monstrous, throbbing machine. 'Some of us have work to do.'

'Is that why you're leaving the office early?'

'Since when are my working hours your concern?'

The biker shrugged.

Magenta's glance swept the car park. Where was the security guard when you needed him? She had been loading up the car with things she intended to finish over the weekend in her own time—not that she was about to explain that to this guy, who looked like he spent his weekends in bed. And not alone.

'You're leaving me?' he demanded as she made a move to continue on her way.

'Somehow I'm managing to drag myself away.'

What was he doing in the car park of Steele Design anyway? Was he a courier? 'Do you have a package?'

His grin made her cheeks blaze red. She had to watch her words in future, Magenta concluded. They were about the same age—maybe he was a year or two older—but his eyes held infinitely more experience. 'If you don't have anything to deliver, this is private property and you should leave.'

He raised an eyebrow.

Oh, good. He was really impressed by her command of the situation.

The biker's self-confidence was making her edgy—that and his manner, which was cool, when she was fuming. Some men were just comfortable in every situation and this man was clearly one of them.

A sharp flurry of snow kept her hurrying along but the man's laugh was warm and sexy on her back. 'What's so urgent you can't spare a moment to chat?' he called.

She stopped and turned to confront him. 'Not that it's any business of yours, but I am going inside to put on the clothes I wear in the gym so I can change the tyre on my car.'

'Can I help you?'

'No.'

Perhaps she should at least have thanked him for the offer.

Now she felt guilty?

Settling the helmet on his head again, he revved the engine. 'You're going?' she said, perversely wanting him to stay.

Powerful shoulders eased in a careless shrug.

Why exactly was she driving him away, when he was the most interesting thing to have happened in a long time? Because she had more sense than to prolong the encounter, Magenta reasoned, crunching snow underfoot as she started on her way again. But, instead of riding off, the man kept pace with her, scuffing his boots on the surface of the road as he kept the engine purring along in neutral. 'Haven't you gone yet?' she demanded.

'I'm waiting to see you in gym clothes.' He grinned.

She huffed at this, all the time trying to work him out. He was dressed too casually to be a businessman and his voice was low and husky with an accent she didn't recognise. Perhaps he was a mature student; there was a college across the road.

'I could give you a lift.'

I bet you could. A face and body like his could give any woman a lift. But something about him warned her that this was a man who could switch in the blink of an eye from humorous and warm to the modern-day equivalent of Genghis Khan—and she'd had all the aggravation she could take for one day.

'You are one stressed-out lady. Don't you ever relax?'

Was he kidding? Who had time to relax? Plus, she shouldn't even think about relaxing while this guy was around. He looked too fit, too dangerous. 'My car is shot. Bust. Broken. What part of that should entice me to relax?'

'Like I said, I'd be happy to give you a lift.'

She might have given his well-packed leathers a thorough

inspection and found them more than to her liking, but she didn't know him from Adam. 'I never accept lifts from strangers,' she informed him, tilting her chin at what she hoped would pass for an unapproachable angle.

'Very wise,' he said, calmly wheeling along at her side.

'Don't you ever give up?'

'Never.'

Her heart was thundering. Why?

She was heading off towards the side entrance and the employee lockers where her gym clothes were stowed, and was looking forward to closing the door on his arrogant face... right up to the moment when he gunned the engine and rode away.

She stared after the streak of black lightning until it disappeared at the end of the road, feeling...wistful.

Well, she'd blown it, so it was no use crying over lost opportunities now.

Had there been something special about him—an instant connection between them? Or was that the wanderings of an exhausted mind?

Far more likely, Magenta decided. The biker could have insisted on fixing her tyre if he'd really wanted to.

Whatever happened to chivalry? Women like her, Magenta concluded, women who accepted equality as their right and who scowled if a man so much as offered to open a door for them.

Having retrieved her gym clothes from her locker, she threw them on, together with a warm jacket and a scarf. Returning to her car, she lifted the cover concealing the spare...

No spare!

She stared in disbelief at the empty space, and then remembered her father saying something about a puncture a few months back. They had matching cars, which at one time Magenta had thought cute. Not today; her father must have told the mechanics to help themselves to her spare and had forgotten to ask them to replace it.

It was her own fault for not checking.

The business was falling down around her ears, she might not even have a job after Christmas and she was crying over a flat tyre. Pressing back against the car, she shut her eyes, waiting for the tears to stop threatening. Finally, having convinced herself it was no use worrying about something she couldn't change, she decided to go inside, get warm and call a cab. Or she could always catch the underground; there was a tube station near her house.

And here came the security guard. Hurrying over to him, Magenta explained she would call someone to come and rescue her car.

When she returned to the office her father was ready to leave, to sign the deal to sell his shares.

'I thought you'd gone,' Clifford Steele complained, checking the angle of his silk tie. 'No family members muddying the water until this new man has settled in and I have his money in the bank—those are the rules.'

'And I was obeying them. I was just loading up the car when I discovered I had a flat. And guess what?' Magenta added dryly. 'I don't have a spare.'

'Call a cab,' her father advised without a flicker of remorse. 'Can't stay,' he added, wrapping a cashmere muffler around his neck. 'I'm off to sign the final papers. Just make sure you're out of here in case Quinn decides to come and take a look at his latest acquisition.'

She heard the note of resentment in her father's voice and kissed his cheek. It couldn't be easy selling out to a younger, more successful man. Clifford Steele might be high-handed, and his extravagance might have brought the company to its knees, but he was her father and she loved him and would do nothing to risk his comfortable retirement. It was up to her to sort the mess out now in an attempt to try and save her colleagues' jobs.

If the new owner allowed her to.

Gray Quinn might not keep her on, Magenta realised anxiously. Thanks to her father's outdated belief that men ran businesses while bricks and mortar provided better security for a woman, she owned the building but not a single voting-share.

'As you're still here, make yourself useful,' her father instructed. 'I'm sure the men would like a cup of coffee before you go. So you're a senior account exec,' he added with impatience when he saw her face. 'But no one makes a cup of coffee like—'

'A well-trained woman?' Magenta suggested, tongue-in-cheek.

'Like you, I was about to say. You work too hard, Magenta, and you take yourself far too seriously. Stress isn't good for a woman your age,' her father commented in his usual tactful manner. 'If you're not careful it will give you wrinkles. You should take a break—get a decent night's sleep.'

'Yes, Dad.' Her father might have stepped straight out of their sixties campaign, when men had a high opinion of themselves and women were still working out how to let them down lightly, Magenta mused wryly. 'That's just the way it is', her father was fond of telling her whenever she complained he was a dinosaur. 'That's just the way *you* are', she always amended fondly.

He had some parting words for her. 'If you'll take my advice, Magenta—which I doubt—you'll make yourself scarce until the new owner is settled in. Quinn will soon lose interest and leave the running of the company to the old guard.'

'Goodbye, Dad.'

Lose interest? That didn't sound like the Gray Quinn Magenta had read about. 'Dynamic and cool under pressure' was how the financial papers described him—not to mention ruthless and tough. Oh yes, and practically invisible. If there was a good photograph of Gray Quinn in existence, he had managed to keep it out of the public eye. Life under her father's autocratic rule had been bad enough, but Quinn was an unknown quantity, and Magenta's major concern was for her colleagues. Of course, if Quinn wanted a clean sweep, he might fire them all—and if he squashed the zing out of the ad agency's creative personnel it would go down anyway.

If Quinn booted her, she would just have to keep an eye on things from the sidelines, Magenta concluded, going to the window to stare out. If she had to remortgage her house and start a new company to keep everyone in work, then she would.

And what exactly was she looking for now? The biker? She should know better.

She did know better, and pulled away.

Turning her back to the window, she huffed wryly. Business might come easily to her, but where men were concerned she had a long history of failure. She didn't have the right chat, the right look—and the guy on the bike would almost certainly know that she hadn't had a date in ages. He looked like some sort of expert where women were concerned. Magenta smiled as she perched on the edge of the desk to call a cab. The famous orgasm was probably a fiction dreamed up by ad men, anyway.

There were no cabs, at least not for an hour or more. Snow and Christmas shoppers were held to account for the shortage of vehicles.

So, the underground it was.

Having checked she had everything she would need to work at home, Magenta called the garage to come and sort out the car and then brought her team into the office for one last discussion. The holidays were almost on them and she wanted everyone to feel confident about launching the campaign in the New Year before she left.

Would she even be coming back? Magenta wondered as her friends filed into the room. She couldn't afford to think like that. She owed it to the team to be positive. She couldn't let them see how worried she was. This wasn't the end of Steele Design, it was a new beginning, she told herself firmly as she announced, 'I'm going to be working at home for the time being.'

'You can't leave the week before Christmas,' Magenta's right arm, Tess, stated flatly.

'I'll be in touch with you the whole time.'

'It's not the same,' Tess argued. 'What about the Christmas party?'

'There are more important things than that—like keeping our jobs?' Magenta suggested when Tess protested. 'And why can't you organise it?' Magenta prodded gently.

'Because you have the magic,' Tess argued.

'I'll be in touch every day, I just won't be physically sitting at my desk—where, apparently,' Magenta added mischievously, 'I might present a threat to Quinn. Yes, I know I'm scary,' she said when the team began to laugh.

While she had them in a good mood she turned the conversation to business. 'You're a fantastic team, and it's crucial that Quinn sees the best of you guys, so I want you to forget about me and concentrate on making a good first impression.'

'Forget about you?' Tess scoffed. 'How are we going to do that when you haven't even given us a theme for the party yet?'

'Glad to hear I've got some uses,' Magenta said dryly, glancing at her wristwatch. She was starting to feel edgy. She had made a promise to her father to keep out of the way, so there wasn't much time for dreaming up ideas for the party. 'Keep it simple,' she instructed herself out loud. 'What about a sixties theme?'

'Brilliant,' Tess agreed. 'We've got half the props already, and you'd look great in a paper dress.'

'Ah...I won't be at the party this year.'

'Well, that's nonsense. What will it be like without you?'

'Much more fun, I should think.' Magenta was remembering how she'd pulled the plug the previous year when she had thought the men in the office were getting a little out of hand. 'I'm only on the end of the phone.'

'I give you twenty-four hours and you'll be back here,' Tess predicted. 'There's too much going on for you to stay away. And there's another thing,' she murmured, drawing Magenta aside. 'I've noticed something different about you this morning. Can't put my finger on it yet, but I will.'

'I don't know what you mean.'

'Ha!' Tess exclaimed. 'You're on the defensive already. You look wary. No,' she argued with herself, 'not wary. You look alert—excited, alive. Yes, that's it. Have you met someone, Magenta?'

'Don't be ridiculous! I'm only worried about the future here.'

'No...' Tess gave a confident shake of her head. 'There's something else—something you're not telling me.'

Maybe her red cheeks had given her away, Magenta thought wryly as the biker flashed into her mind.

'It's nothing to be ashamed of if you've met someone you like,' Tess insisted.

'But I haven't,' Magenta argued—too heatedly, she realised now.

CHAPTER TWO

TESS hurried to reassure her. 'I know you're worried about the company, and what's going to happen under the new owner, but you're entitled to a private life, Magenta. In fact, as your friend I'm going to be blunt about this—you *need* a private life.'

Magenta paused before continuing. 'All right. This is going to sound ridiculous…'

'Try me.'

Tess was waiting but, though she worked with words for a living, Magenta was suddenly struck dumb. How could she explain the trembling inside her, or the excitement, the awareness, even the outlandish suspicion that she had met her soul mate this morning? The biker had caught her at the worst possible moment and yet with his arrival it was as if everything had brightened. As if the world had suddenly come into sharp focus—and in a freezing-cold car park, of all places. How romantic!

The fact remained, it was as if the sun had shone down just on her, as if her life had opened up to a multi-coloured carousel of opportunity.

If she'd had the courage to seize it, which she clearly she hadn't. 'There was a guy this morning in the car park.'

'I knew it.'

'Shh.' Magenta glanced round, but no one was listening; they were too busy fighting over the choice of music for the party. 'It was nothing—just a good-looking guy. Not my type at all, and he wasn't remotely interested. So now you know.'

'But he excited you?'

'He certainly did something.'

'He made you tingle. He made you feel alive.'

'You're a romantic, Tess. He made me angry.'

'You shouted at him?' Tess frowned.

'I gave him a piece of my mind, yes.'

'And how did he react?'

'He laughed at me.'

'But that's wonderful!' Tess exclaimed. 'What a start.'

'There is no start, it was just an episode.'

'And episodes have sequels.'

'Not this one, Tess.'

'You never know, he may come back. He's seen you now—how could he resist? And when a man laughs with you, well, that's the start of intimacy, in my book.'

'It is?'

'Don't you know anything?'

'Not much,' Magenta confessed. 'After the rush of gold-diggers when I was in my first flush of youth, all the likely contenders lost interest.'

'Only because you frightened them away, dragon lady.'

'They weren't worth keeping.'

'And this guy's a keeper?'

'For someone, definitely, but not me.'

'Why not? What's wrong with you?'

'It's not even worth discussing,' Magenta said wryly. 'He's not going to ask me out on a date. I don't expect I'll ever see him again. It was just a chance encounter that made some sort of ridiculous impression on me because I was feeling tired and vulnerable, and—'

'Lacking in confidence where the mating game is concerned,' Tess supplied. 'Just promise me one thing, Magenta—

if you do see him again, don't shout at him. Try a smile next time.'

They both laughed as Tess demonstrated how to do it.

'Come on,' Magenta said, turning back to the room. 'I need to call this meeting to order or the Mighty Quinn will be here and my father will never speak to me again. So, are we good?' she asked her team. 'Does everyone like the theme for the party?'

'Can we share out the sixties samples for costumes and accessories?' one of the girls asked her.

'Of course. Just help yourselves.'

Magenta was relieved her idea had gone down so well. Everyone needed a boost. They were all on edge wondering what changes the new owner would bring, and the sixties theme allowed them to indulge their fantasies and forget about work for a while. Her team had really been infected by the sixties bug, with quite a few of them trialling the fashions of the time. The sixties styling really suited Tess, Magenta noticed now, with her smoky eyes, long, curving fringe and high ponytail, Tess looked fabulous.

'I still can't believe you're not going to be here when the new boss arrives,' Tess said, seeing she had Magenta's attention.

'I'll leave that pleasure to you. All right, go on,' Magenta said, seeing Tess was bursting to tell her something. 'You've heard some gossip about him,' she guessed. 'What is it?'

'Girls!' Tess exclaimed dramatically as she turned to face the room. 'Will you enlighten this poor innocent about our new owner, or shall I?'

No one was going to deny Tess that pleasure, Magenta suspected.

She was right. Raising a carefully drawn eyebrow, Tess explained, 'They call him the Mighty Quinn because according to the gossip mags—' and here she paused '—Gray Quinn isn't just a giant in business, if you take my meaning.'

Magenta pretended to be shocked. 'But no one knows him, no one's seen him. How do they know?'

'Oh, come on,' Tess protested. 'Don't tell me you don't like a little mystery in your life? And if he's built—'

'Tess, this is a professional environment.' But Magenta had started to laugh. 'Okay, so maybe we have to get him into some tight-fitting flares to find out.'

'There, I knew you wouldn't leave us,' Tess declared. 'You have to stay and see him now. You can't resist.'

Magenta felt a frisson of alarm. She wasn't an experienced girl-about-town like Tess. Business was her comfort zone; it would be far better if she wasn't here if Quinn was some sort of lady-killer. She felt confident behind a desk—writing, dreaming, imagining how other people might react to an advertisement, to life—but when it came to herself…

'Look at this,' Tess said, pushing a magazine across the table. 'And then tell me you're going to stay away from the office while Quinn settles in.'

'There's not much to see,' Magenta complained, though her body reacted strangely to what was little more than a shot of a man's back. What was so arousing about that? For some weird reason, her body disagreed.

Quinn was obviously in a hurry to get wherever he'd been going, Magenta registered, studying the grainy print to try and fathom out her reaction to it. And then she got a bolt of something totally inappropriate for a woman who by her own admission was hardly sexually experienced. Quinn's height, the imposing width of his shoulders, the way he held himself—everything appealed to her. Quinn was different from most men in that he was taut, powerful and exuded confidence, as if he were ready for anything. He looked like the type of man who inspired confidence in others, too.

He wouldn't even look at her, Magenta reassured herself, releasing a long, shivering breath. There were so many pretty girls in the world, quite a few of whom worked here at Steele

Design. Why would a man like Quinn look at an old maid like her?

Theirs would be a match made in hell, she convinced herself, pushing the magazine back to Tess. Imagine adding a man like that to her workload!

'What do you know about Quinn, Magenta?' one of the younger girls asked her. 'We know you did lots of research on him when you started to prepare this project to entice him to invest in Steele Design.'

'I did,' Magenta admitted. 'But I was never able to find any proper photographs. I'm surprised Tess found this.' She glanced again at the magazine. 'I gather Quinn's celebrity-averse. And no wonder, judging by the gossip you've heard about him. A man like that must prize his privacy above everything else. I do know he was orphaned at an early age, and that he dragged himself up by his bootstraps, but that's about it. Oh, and he doesn't suffer fools gladly.'

'At all,' Tess amended, shooting a warning glance around the circle of suddenly concerned faces.

'Which is why you have to be on your mettle whether I'm here or not,' Magenta stressed. Smoothing back her long, dark hair, she wound it into the casual chignon she customarily wore at the office, securing it with a silver clip. 'And don't forget that, unless Quinn sacks me, I'll be back in the New Year when we'll make our final presentation to him as a team.'

'Sacks you?' Tess pulled a face. 'I haven't read that he's crazy.'

'But he may not want a member of the *old guard* working for him, as my father calls us. Here are some documents I drew up—where we are with each campaign et cetera. Make sure he gets them, will you, Tess?'

'Of course I will…' But Tess still looked worried. 'Do you *have* to go?'

'I can't risk screwing up Dad's deal.'

'Well, at least you don't have to worry about the documents. I'll see Quinn gets them.'

'Thank you.' Magenta turned to go. But she should have known Tess hadn't finished with her yet.

'And if you change your mind about the party…'

'I only wish I could.' The end-of-year party was important, but nowhere near as important as keeping Magenta's team in work. The last thing she wanted was to alienate Quinn, or have him think she was trying to split the team's loyalty. She hoped she had made a persuasive case for keeping all her colleagues on in the documents she'd given Tess. To add a little weight to that hope, she had drafted an outline for the next campaign, centred on products she knew Quinn wanted to push and which she hoped would keep his interest in the company going forward.

'You *can't* leave us,' Tess stressed discreetly as Magenta prepared to go. 'You're the heart of the team.'

'You'll do just fine without me—and, anyway, I haven't gone yet. Let's see how it goes. Quinn isn't a fool. Just keep doing what you're doing, and he won't be able to let any of you go.'

But Magenta started fretting before she left the room. The promise to her father counted highly with her, but it went against the grain to walk out on her friends. Her father had his money now and wanted nothing more to do with the company, whereas her colleagues were all desperate to keep their jobs. Maybe Tess was right; maybe she wouldn't be able to stay away.

When Magenta got down to the car park it was full of recovery vehicles with red lights flashing and men in high-vis jackets.

Why was nothing ever straightforward? Magenta wondered, urging herself to remain calm as the mechanics explained to her that, as hers was a vintage car, they couldn't repair it now but would have to order a tyre. They were going to recover the vehicle and keep it in the garage over Christmas and she could collect it some time in the New Year. No, they couldn't be more specific than that, the mechanic in charge told her, scratching his head.

Pulling up her collar against a sudden squall of icy wind, Magenta thanked the men for turning out in such diabolical weather and insisted on giving each of them a crisp new note. Why shouldn't someone enjoy their day?

Wrapping her arms around her body to keep warm, she watched as her car was loaded onto the transporter. She was just bending down to retrieve her bag and briefcase when a familiar roar made her jump, and a familiar boot stamping down by her feet made her scowl.

'Don't tell me,' she managed as the biker lifted off his helmet. 'You didn't get me the first time around, so you've come back to finish me off with a heart attack?'

'Your heart's safe from me.'

Oh...

Was she supposed to feel quite so disappointed? Magenta's brain raced as the biker lifted one ebony eyebrow, sending a tidal wave of hot, feral lust rushing through her veins. Removing one protective leather glove, the man stretched out his hand for her to shake.

'You surely don't expect me to shake your hand after you've frightened me half to death, not once but twice?'

He grinned. 'You're not that feeble, I'm sure. But my apologies, if I frightened you.'

The mock bow made her heart thunder into action. But what exactly did he find so funny?

'Something tells me we're going to be seeing a lot of each other,' the biker said, closing one warm, strong hand around Magenta's frozen fingers.

Yeah, right. In your dreams, she thought.

CHAPTER THREE

As THE biker dismounted his machine and straightened up, Magenta felt her cheeks fire red. He was a lot taller than she had expected and had the type of shoulders that blotted out the light. She had to fight the desire to give him a comprehensive twice-over. She already knew he was an amazing-looking man and that tight black leathers were no respecters of female sensibilities. She dropped her gaze as a dangerous stare levelled on her face.

'Lost your voice?' The voice was low and amused, husky and compelling.

And leather didn't conceal or contain, it stretched and moulded shapes lovingly...

'Well? Have you?' he prompted.

No, but she had been struck by one too many thunderbolts in a single day, Magenta concluded, whipping her head up to stare the man in the eyes. He curved a smile in response that threw her totally, a smile that made his eyes crinkle attractively at the corners.

'I'm glad you think this is funny,' she said, covering her growing feeling of awkwardness with a scowl. 'I don't care who you are, what you just did was dangerous.' Now she sounded like his headmistress and felt old enough to hold the post.

That grin spread from his mouth to his eyes, making her wonder if he'd read that thought.

'You look to me like you badly need a ride.'
Where had that thought come from?

She wished she had the guts to throw him the same grin he had given her earlier. But no, this was how she was, clumsy with men, which made her grumpy and defensive. She might be heavily into studying the sixties for the ad campaign, but it would never occur to her to embrace the concept of free love. And from what she'd seen to date nothing about love was free, Magenta reflected as the biker continued to study her with amused interest.

'I thought I might come back and see if you still needed rescuing.'

'Not then and not now.'

'A man is programmed to play the white knight—it's built into the genes.'

The only thing that was built into his jeans was a warning that she was out of her depth. 'I can look after myself, thank you.'

'And so you prove this by standing out here, freezing your butt off?'

Just the mention of her butt caused her body to heat. 'I haven't been standing outside all this time. And, anyway, I'm going home now.'

'And how do you intend to do that?'

'On the underground, or in a cab.'

'You'll be lucky.'

'Meaning?'

'Delays on the line; buses bulging at the seams. And there's not a taxi to found. Not a free one, at least.'

She tried not to notice how beautiful the biker's eyes were. They were aquamarine with steely grey rims around the iris, the whites very white and his lashes completely wasted on a man. While his tongue was firmly lodged in his cheek, Magenta suspected. 'What are you?' she demanded. 'Some sort of information clerk for the city of London?

'Just observant. Have you worked up the courage to take a ride with me yet?'

Unfortunately, he was right. She could stay here and freeze or she could take her chances with public transport. But hadn't she been lectured on the dangers of taking life too seriously? Shouldn't she at least consider the biker's offer?

Absolutely not.

She turned her back, only to find herself checking the road for black ice. The mystery biker might be the most infuriating, the most arrogant, overbearing and impossible man she'd ever met, but the thought of finding him mashed up in a gutter made her heart race with fear for him. 'Take care—it's slippery,' she mumbled and, putting her head down, she marched towards the exit.

Wheeling his bike in front of her, he stopped dead.

'What are you doing?' Magenta demanded.

'I don't take no for an answer.' His eyes glinted with laughter.

'I can see that. Does everything amuse you?' she demanded, stepping round his bike.

'You make me smile.'

She kept on walking, but as she dragged her jacket a little closer it occurred to Magenta that she was perhaps being a little ungracious. 'If you're looking for someone…'

The biker's eyes glinted.

'I'm just trying to say, if I can help you in any way…'

'Get on the bike.'

No! Yes. What should she do? She had been fascinated by the beacon of freedom women lit in the sixties and talked a good battle when it came to championing the cause—but did she ever seize the moment and take action? Or did she always play it safe?

Too damn safe. 'Helmet?'

The biker produced a spare and then patted the seat behind him.

'You're very sure of yourself, aren't you?' she commented as she buckled it on.

'Sure of you. You can't resist a challenge, can you?'

'And how do you know that?'

He shrugged.

'The helmet seems like it might fit—'

'Then climb on board.'

The husky voice suggested a chastity belt might be a useful piece of kit too.

'Before I change my mind…' He revved the engine.

'Are you always so forceful?'

'Yes.'

The master of the one word answer drowned out the demented timpanist in charge of her heart by taking the revs up to danger level. And now she took a proper look at his monster machine she wasn't even sure she could climb on board, as the biker put it. Did her legs even stretch that wide?

'Chicken?' The smile was masculine and mocking.

'I am not.' She played for time. 'That's a Royal Enfield, isn't it?'

'You know motorbikes?'

Her attention flew to a very sexy mouth. 'I know the brand, thanks to my research into the sixties,' she said primly. She might have known someone as cool as the biker wouldn't ride a pimped-up, over-hyped modern machine. The Enfield was a serious motorbike for serious riders. Big and black, it was vibrating insistently between his leather-clad thighs.

And would soon be vibrating between hers.

No way was she climbing on board.

And she was getting home…how?

Call a cab, the sensible side of her brain suggested. There had to be an empty cab somewhere in the whole of London.

'You are chicken,' the biker insisted, slanting an amused glance Magenta's way.

She laughed dismissively, longing for a way out. But she'd done 'sensible' all her life, and look where that had got her.

'Well?'

'Forbidden fruit' sprang to mind when she looked at him—fruit that was so close, so ripe and so dangerously delicious, she could practically taste it on her tongue. 'How do I know I'll be safe with you?'

'You don't.'

Her pulse raced. But then, she reasoned, it was only a lift home—why the fuss? 'Shouldn't you know my address before we set off?'

'So, tell me.'

She found herself doing so even as she wondered how his strong white teeth would feel if he used them to lightly nip her skin.

'It's time to get on the bike,' he prompted. 'I've no intention of running out of fuel while I wait for you to make up your mind.'

'Could you take my briefcase and stow it for me, please?'

'My pleasure, ma'am.' He held out his hand.

'I suppose I should thank you,' she added belatedly.

'I suppose you should,' he agreed.

'If you're sure it's not out of your way?'

'I'm sure.'

This man would be equally certain about every decision he made. He'd be just as decisive when he left her standing here freezing her butt off, as he'd so elegantly put it, on the basis of her extreme cowardice.

'Would you like some help?' he said, looking on in bemusement as she started hopping into position.

All she had to do was throw one leg across his seat. How hard could that be? 'I'm fine, thank you.'

After one final heave and a lot of unladylike wriggling, she was finally in position—which meant close up to the biker. She tried to shuffle back a bit to maintain the proprieties, but the moment he kicked the stand away, released the brake and gunned the engine she launched herself at him, wrapping her arms as tightly as she could around his waist.

A waist without an ounce of fat on it, Magenta registered, but an awful lot of muscle, and if there was a way to ride pillion behind the biker without allowing her body to mould with his—thankfully, it had escaped her.

By the time they joined the heavy London traffic, she was pretty familiar with the biker's back and the way his thick hair escaped the helmet to caress the collar on his jacket. She was so familiar she had even started shivering…with cold, Magenta told herself firmly. Having consigned her safety to the hands of a man she hardly knew, that was more than enough risk to take in one day.

He really knew how to handle a bike and wove in and out of the congested streets of London like a man who really knew what he was doing, while Magenta was increasingly conscious of the insistent vibrations beneath her. It was almost a disappointment when they rolled up outside her neatly manicured town house. Dismounting the bike shakily, she removed her helmet and shook out her long, black hair.

'That's quite a transformation, lady,' the biker commented as he lifted off his helmet to stare at her.

'You think so?' Magenta laughed as she retrieved her clip as it fell to the ground. She couldn't remember feeling so carefree in a long time. Her hair had been blown to blazes, like the rest of her—and it felt great. *She* felt great. 'Thanks.'

'My pleasure.' His face creased in the now-familiar grin.

Did she imagine the curtains in nearby houses were twitching? For once she didn't care what anyone thought. So she had ridden home on the bike of a tough-looking guy, ditching the power suit and the high-heeled shoes along the way. Short of stripping naked and leaping on top of him in the middle of the street, she was committing no crime.

'Coffee?' she said, still in the throws of enthusiasm. It

seemed only polite. And when would an opportunity like this come round again?

The man's laser gaze was every bit as astonishing as she remembered; she was sure he was going to say, 'why not?' But what he actually said was, 'I should get back.'

'Of course…' What was she thinking?

Where overtures towards good-looking guys were concerned, she was somewhat out of practice, Magenta conceded. But, as this wasn't an overture—not even close—but merely a polite invitation to enjoy a hot drink before making a return journey in the cold, she had nothing to worry about, did she? 'Genuine Blue Mountain coffee.'

'You make it hard to refuse,' he admitted, slanting a smoky grey-green stare her way.

Impossible, hopefully. Having tasted danger, she wanted more. 'So?' she pressed. Pulling out the house keys, she dangled them in front of him.

'I have to get back.'

Of course he did. 'Another time,' she said brightly, swallowing down her disappointment. 'You've done more than enough for me already. Goodness knows how far you've come out of your way.'

'Not far.'

Tess would be furious with her; she didn't even know his name. But she couldn't hold him here while she cross-questioned him without inviting further humiliation. 'It's been good meeting you.'

'And you.' He grinned.

By the time she had lifted her hand to wave him off, he'd gone.

CHAPTER FOUR

WHY did her house seem so quiet and empty, when it never had before?

Because of the biker, Magenta concluded. With his larger than life personality, he didn't even need to speak to command attention; he just had to *be*.

Having changed her clothes, and kicked off her shoes with relief, she picked the mail up and headed for the kitchen. The phone stopped her dead. She picked it up.

'Magenta Steele?' The voice was crisp, deep and very masculine. 'Gray Quinn here.'

Magenta's heart rolled over. 'Gray…'

'Most people call me Quinn.' There was a hint of a smile in the voice, but not enough to reassure. 'I'm in the office tying up some loose ends. I'd like to see you for a discussion on your position going forward with the company first thing tomorrow morning.'

'But my father said—'

'Your father doesn't head up Steele Design now. I do. Nine o'clock okay with you?'

'Of course…' A chill ran through her. Quinn might be a sexy charmer, according to office gossip, but she'd just encountered the Genghis Khan side of him.

'I'll see you tomorrow, Magenta—nine o'clock sharp.'

And it wasn't a suggestion but an order, Magenta gathered as the line cut.

Coffee was needed. The temptation to go straight back to the office to gauge the effect Quinn was having on everyone else was almost impossible to resist. She was worried about her colleagues and felt uncomfortable leaving them.

Plus she had work she could do better at the office, she persuaded herself, and if she got through enough of it her team could have more time off for Christmas shopping. She would get Tess to ring her when the coast was clear.

Now the decision was made, she was all fired up. Forget taking a subtle approach where Quinn was concerned; if she waited until he was bedded in, as her father had suggested, it might be too late to save her friends' jobs. Abandoning the idea of coffee, she ran upstairs to take a shower and freshen up.

Now new doubts set in. Even if Tess rung her when Quinn left the office, there was still the possibility he might return and find her there. The thought of meeting him filled Magenta with excitement, but it also filled her with the type of self-doubt that had always plagued her where men were concerned. She would need a lot more than a freshen-up before she ran into Quinn—a full-body overhaul was called for.

Guided by the horribly honest mirrors in her bathroom, it soon became apparent that she was up against the clock in more ways than one. She would just have to make whatever repairs she could in the short time available.

Collecting up the sixties products she had been hoarding to fuel her imagination for the campaign, she rested the plastic crate on top of the linen basket and started rummaging inside. A queen-sized razor; not a bad place to start.

And what was this? *Myriad sparkles of dewy fragrance will embrace your body in a haze of desire at just the touch of a button…*

A love potion? Well, she could certainly do with some of that.

But after her shower, she decided, stepping beneath the steaming spray.

She had a whole range of retro products in the shower too. She had definitely been infected by the sixties bug. Magenta smiled wryly as she soaped down and thought about Quinn. What would he be like?

That was the only excuse her imagination needed to go crazy. There was only one thing that could make this self-indulgent shower any better, and that was sharing it with Quinn—not that she would; not in the real world. She was better off sticking to work and researching the sixties.

'Soap-on-a-rope, come here to me,' Magenta crooned, capturing the hippopotamus-shaped soap currently swinging on a cord from her shower head.

She glanced through the open door towards her bed, realising how tired she was. The temptation was to just fall into bed after her shower and dream about Quinn, put a face to that grainy back-view in the magazine… Perhaps she'd wake up to discover she had a really big share-holding in the business—power and some cards to play.

But that wasn't going to happen…

Turning her face up to the spray, Magenta knew she would have to take a more conventional route by producing some of her best work and by working her thermal socks off.

Turning the shower off, she grabbed a couple of towels and returned to the bedroom, where a spear of inspiration struck. Why not go the whole hog and dress in sixties clothes? Quite a few of her colleagues had already adopted the fashions and the look, so why not join them?

They always banded together at this time of year and had such fun—decorating the office, sneaking out for warm, full-fat mince pies with thick globs of cream on top—and this year the sixties vibe was adding a special frisson to the holiday celebrations.

She was drying her hair absent-mindedly with a towel as

she started flicking through her wardrobe. Like everyone else in the creative team, she had been scouring the vintage shops for examples of sixties clothing, and had struck gold with a form-fitting cream wool dress. Sliding it off the hanger, she laid it on the bed.

Suppliers had rushed to offer samples of their retro products when Magenta had let it be known that she would be running a high-profile campaign, so she had plenty of accessories to choose from. Fortunately, it hadn't been all mini-skirts and hot-pants in the sixties. There had been the hippies in their flowing, get-em-off-quick clothes, the shock-frock dolly-birds in mini-skirts, as well as a more elegant side to the era. This was where Magenta felt comfortable—though it was the underwear she was supposed to wear beneath these stylish clothes that made her laugh. *Break out of your little-girl body when you're feeling in a big-girl mood*, ran the legend on one pack of matching bra and girdle.

Well, she wasn't a little girl, but she was definitely in a big-girl mood, Magenta decided, conjuring up a vision of Quinn as she broke the seal on the packaging.

It was almost impossible not to think about the new owner of the business, Magenta realised, opening the towel she had wrapped around her body to give her twenty-eight-year-old figure a critical review. She was sitting on the bed facing the dressing-table mirror and she sat up straight immediately. Would he like real women with real bellies, or would his tastes run to something younger and slimmer? Not that she could do much about it in the short time at her disposal. And why worry when her naked body was in zero danger of becoming an issue between them?

She picked up another pack and studied it. *What do you wear under your action-wear? Action Underwear, of course...*

But there wasn't going to be any action.

She put it down, picking up something called the *Concentrate* girdle.

Concentrate on what? Holding her stomach in the whole time?

I don't think so.

And she certainly didn't need the *Little Fibber* bra—one of the only benefits of getting a little older and a little rounder, Magenta thought dryly, tossing the formidable-looking steel-girder-style bra to one side. Strange to think the so-called liberated women of the twenty-first century made so little of her breasts. Breasts were never flaunted at the office in case you were thought of as brainless, as if having lactating glands in common with a cow meant you automatically shared the same IQ. Perhaps that was the reason she had never worn form-fitting clothes to the office before, though she doubted a man as focused on business as Quinn appeared to be would even notice.

She hunted for some sheer tights in her drawer, only to discard them in favour of stockings. Underpinnings were everything, an actress friend had told her—those and shoes. If you didn't get that right, you stood no chance of playing a period piece convincingly.

She picked up another box and quickly disposed of it with an unwelcome shiver of arousal. *Damsel in Undress* was a definite no-no. The slightest hint to a man like Quinn that she was adopting a compliant 'men rule' mindset to go along with her sixties outfit, and she'd be in big trouble. He'd already given her a flavour of his management style. Gray Quinn definitely didn't need any encouragement. He was shaping up to be the original alpha-male. No, this was one occasion when she would be sixties on the outside and bang up to date in her head. But she would consent to wear a provocative cone-shaped bra to achieve the authentic hourglass shape—not forgetting control pants for the belly problem.

And a suspender-belt and stockings were fun…

Having dressed, she slipped on her stiletto heels and immediately felt different. She walked differently too. She tried a few steps up and down the bedroom and found herself sashaying like a famous actress in a hot sixties television programme. She smiled, thinking her actress friend had been right. The shoes and the clothes were like a costume that put her right back in the era, and that was fun.

It was even more fun when she started on the make-up—pale foundation and big, smoky eyes outlined so that they appeared even larger. And some *Un-lipstick*, as it was called, in Shiver Shiver pink.

She certainly shivered as she tasted it. What would Quinn make of that?

Not that he would ever get a chance to find out, Magenta told herself firmly. This was all about dressing up and fantasy. Pressing her lips together, she blotted them in the manner prescribed on the pack and then applied a second coat.

Not bad.

She was ready.

Ready for pretty much anything, Magenta decided as she checked her appearance one last time in the mirror.

She waited for Tess's call and when it came she travelled to the office by taxi to find all the lights were out. Just as Tess had promised, there was no sign of Quinn—exactly what she wanted. Well, it would be, once she had stifled her disappointment. All that effort put into grooming for nothing.

At least she could concentrate on work, Magenta told herself firmly. This was a great opportunity to put the finishing touches to the campaign. Having set out her papers on the large desk in her office, she slipped the lock on the door, feeling safer that way in an empty building. She'd make some coffee later to keep herself awake.

She was halfway through drafting a strap line for a sixties hairpiece when she had to stop. She could hardly keep her eyes open and just couldn't get it right: *the hair fashion that goes on when you go out...*

And drops off when you least expect it to?

Magenta examined the yard-long ponytail made out of synthetic hair and tossed it aside. Some of the products being used to inject fun into the campaign were odd, but this was downright ugly. Surely no self-respecting woman would want to wear a hair-tugger on top of her head that weighed a ton, looked gross and at a guess took a whole card of hair grips to hold in place? If you weren't bald when you started your evening out, you certainly would be by the end of it.

And yet it was a genuine sixties product, Magenta mused, leaning her cheek against her folded arms as she stared at the unappealing hairpiece and waiting for inspiration to strike. She'd been so enthusiastic up to now, seeing only the good, the fun and the innovation of the sixties. But, realistically, how many other things about that time would have got right up her nose?

'Magenta...Magenta! Wake up!'

'What's wrong?' Magenta started with alarm as someone grabbed hold of her arm and shook her awake. Well dressed in sixties style, the girl looked smart and bright—and totally unfamiliar. Magenta felt like she had the hangover from hell—and, not having had a drop to drink, that was a serious concern. 'How long have I been asleep?' Her neck suddenly didn't seem strong enough to lift her ridiculously heavy head from the desk.

'Magenta, you have to get out of here now.'

'Why? Is there a fire?'

'Worse—Quinn,' the girl explained with what sounded like panic in her voice. 'He mustn't find you here.'

'Why not?' Magenta stared in bewilderment around her office, which seemed to have been cleared of all her creature comforts while she'd been asleep. But it wasn't just the flowers, the coffee machine, the bottles of water or the family photographs that were missing. 'Hey, where's my laptop?' she said, shooting up. 'Has there been a robbery?'

'Magenta, I don't know what you're talking about, but I do know you have to get out of here now.'

'All right, all right!' Magenta exclaimed as the girl took her by the arm and physically dragged her towards the door. 'I'm sure I locked this door last night.'

'I used my key.' The girl shook a spare set in her face.

'What's the rush? I'll need my mobile phone, and where's my tote, my handbag, my briefcase?' Magenta demanded, glancing back at the vastly changed room.

'No more questions,' her new friend hissed frantically, tugging at Magenta's arm. 'We don't have time. Quinn will be here any minute.'

A multitude of thoughts and impressions were slowly percolating through Magenta's sluggish brain. This was a new girl, possibly someone Quinn had brought in. She seemed nice, though, confusingly, she seemed to know Magenta when Magenta was certain they had never met before. 'Did Quinn get my list?' she said, clinging on to priorities while her brain sorted itself out.

'What list? You didn't give me a list.'

'No, that's right—I gave it to Tess.'

'Tess?'

This girl didn't know Tess? 'Sorry, uh…'

'Nancy,' the girl supplied, looking at her with real concern. 'Magenta, are you sure you're okay?'

'Yes, I'm fine.' This was growing stranger by the minute; if she hadn't felt so heavy-headed she would have been faster off the mark. 'I gave a list of the list of things Quinn should implement immediately to one of the girls in the office.'

Nancy huffed. 'If you had given me a list like that, I would have seriously lost it on purpose.'

'Has Quinn been bullying you?' She forgot her own confusion; bullying in the office was one thing she wouldn't stand, and Magenta's concerns soared when Nancy refused to answer almost as if she was frightened of being overheard. 'Well, no one's going to bully you while I'm around—especially not Quinn.'

Nancy hummed and started tugging on Magenta's arm again. 'I'm not joking, Magenta, we have to get out of here.'

'But where do you want me to go?' This had been Magenta's office since—well, she could hardly remember; it had been hers for so long now.

'You work in the typing pool, remember?' Nancy told her urgently, poking her head out of the door to check the coast was clear.

'The typing pool?' Magenta laughed. 'Is this some joke of Quinn's to get us all in the right mood for the sixties campaign?'

Nancy gave her a funny look.

'To be more accurate, you *used to* work in the typing pool,' she finally replied, nudging Magenta towards the door. 'The guy who ran the place before hotshot Quinn arrived from the States took his office manager with him, so Quinn promoted you.'

'Why didn't Quinn text me? And what's this?' Magenta demanded as Nancy bundled her towards a mean little desk set to one side of her office door—a door she now noticed with outrage that already bore the legend, 'Gray Quinn'.

'This is your desk now, Magenta,' Nancy explained. 'It's a great improvement to the typing pool, don't you think?'

'Do you want to hear what I think? No. I didn't think so,' Magenta agreed as Nancy shook her head. 'I don't know what's happening around here, but this isn't my desk—and Quinn definitely can't take over my office.'

'But, Magenta, you used to work in the typing pool—you've never *had* your own office,' Nancy insisted, looking increasingly concerned about Magenta's state of mind. 'Don't you remember anything?'

Magenta swept a hand across her eyes as if hoping everything would change back again by the time she opened them again. But, to make things worse, people she didn't even know were staring at her as if she was the one who was mad.

But how could this have happened? She gazed around and felt her anger rising. Quinn had to be some sort of monumental chauvinist; men occupied all the private offices while the women had been relegated to old-fashioned typewriters— either in the typing pool, where they sat in rows behind a partition as if they were at school, or at similar desks to this one outside the office doors. Ready to do their master's bidding, Magenta presumed angrily. She remembered her father telling her how it used to be for the majority of female office workers in the sixties. 'Why are all the girls typing?' she asked Nancy in a heated whisper.

'It's their job!' Nancy said, frowning.

'But why aren't they working on the campaign?' Magenta noticed now that many of the women, some of whose faces were adorned with heavy-framed, upswept spectacles, were pretending not to look at her.

'What campaign?' Nancy queried, stepping back as a keen teen brushed passed her.

'Wow, Magenta, you look really choice!'

'I do?' Magenta spun on her heels as the young man she had never seen before gave her a rather too comprehensive once-over. 'Why, thank you…?'

'Jackson,' Nancy supplied, having cottoned on to the fact that Magenta needed all the help she could get.

'Jackson.' Magenta raised a brow. 'Stop staring at your Auntie Magenta and go find yourself a girlfriend.'

Jackson laughed as if Magenta could always be relied upon to say something funny. 'You're a gas, baby.'

Had Quinn changed all the personnel? Of course, he was

perfectly entitled to, Magenta reasoned. Quinn ran the show now. But what had happened to her friends? And what had happened to their working environment?

So many questions stacked up in her mind, with not a single answer to one of them that made sense.

CHAPTER FIVE

'Look, Magenta, I don't want to rush you,' Nancy said in a way that clearly said that was exactly what she wanted to do. 'But Quinn's only slipped out for an eleven o'clock appointment.'

'So what?' Magenta said impatiently. 'He's got a damn nerve.' She was still looking round, trying to take everything in. She could understand Quinn wanting to live the sixties in order to give the campaign that final fizz of authenticity—hadn't she done the same thing herself? But didn't he know there was such a thing as going too far? 'Nancy, what's been going on here?'

'The usual?' Following her glance, Nancy gazed around the office.

'The usual,' Magenta repeated grimly. 'Is it usual to remove the computers?'

'The what?'

'Okay, so Quinn's got you playing his game,' Magenta said. 'I can understand that you don't want to lose your job—I'm just thinking of all the expense involved in putting this right again—' She had already reasoned that the reorganisation of the office would have been fairly easy if Quinn had copied the layout from the old photographs on the wall, but there were other things she couldn't account for. There was a different feel to the place, never mind the look, which was dated, a little drab and definitely not the right environment to encourage cutting-edge design work. She thought it boring, not to mention inhospitable. There were different phones too, but it was the ergonomically unhelpful furniture that really concerned her—and single glazing? Had Quinn gone mad? Never mind the expense, what about condensation? Cold? If people were uncomfortable at work, productivity would suffer. Didn't Quinn know anything?

And there was a different smell too...

Cigarette smoke?

'Nancy!' Magenta exclaimed with increased urgency.

'Are you all right, Magenta?' Glancing round, Nancy grabbed a chair and tried to press Magenta into it.

'I'm fine.' She was anything but fine. What had happened here? Had Quinn got people in to dress the offices like a sixties stage-set? And how was it possible she had slept through those changes? But it wasn't just the noise element that concerned her; these changes were too thorough, too perfect, too convincing...

Magenta's throat dried. This wasn't some office team-building exercise. This was reality. This was reality for Nancy and for all the people here. It was Magenta who was out of sync. She must have fallen down the rabbit hole, like Alice, while she'd been asleep and landed in the sixties. And now the shock of being trapped inside a dream was only exceeded by her dread of meeting Quinn. From what she'd gathered, he was just the sort of man who would slot right into the sixties, where men ruled. Quinn obviously thought they did.

Magenta took a few steadying breaths while Nancy looked on anxiously. Magenta's heart was pounding uncontrollably, but whatever had happened she would have to manage it.

She looked as much a part of the sixties as everyone else in the office, Magenta reassured herself, with her carefully made-up face, perfect hair and vintage cream wool dress. Though you could have bounced bullets off her underwear, it did outline her shape to the point where her breasts were outrageously prominent. That, believe it or not, was the fashion. It could best be described as 'sex in your face'. No wonder Jackson had commented; she should have known better than to dress like this, but had done so innocently. Back in the real world, it had made her feel sexy—and after the encounter with the biker she had wanted to prove to herself that she still could feel that way. Now she realised drawing attention to herself in a sixties office was asking for trouble.

But, on the plus side, she had been researching the era for quite some time, so even locked into this bizarre dream she wasn't entirely out on a limb. She could even accept and be a little reassured by the fact that the dream seemed to be influenced by her research; there was certainly plenty of raw material here. Although quite how the summer of love, the sexual revolution and the Whisky a Go Go, the first disco in America—which just happened to be Quinn's homeland— would manifest themselves remained to be seen.

She would have to rely on what she knew if she was going to anticipate and avoid some of the problems, Magenta concluded. She would draw on that knowledge now—and her first action would be to open all the windows and let the smoke out.

Predictably everyone complained that it was too cold. 'Well, you can't smoke in here,' Magenta insisted. 'It's against the law.'

'Since when?' one of the younger guys asked, swinging his arm around her waist to drag her close so she had no alternative but to inhale his foul-smelling breath.

'And that is too,' she informed him, removing his searching hand from her tightly sculpted rear end.

'Ooh.' He turned to his friends to pull a mocking face. 'What got into your bed this morning, Miss Steele?'

'No one?' another man suggested, to raucous jeers.

'We all know what's wrong with you, ice maiden.'

'Cut it out!' Magenta said angrily. 'I'm not in the mood.'

'Apparently, you never are,' one of the men murmured to his colleagues in a stage whisper.

As if that were the cue for the main player to enter the scene, the double doors at the far end of the office swung open and every head swivelled in that direction. Some of the women even stood at their desks as if royalty was about to enter the room. To say Magenta was stunned by this reaction wouldn't even come close. 'What the...?'

'Quinn,' Nancy told her tensely, hurrying away.

Magenta turned to say something to Nancy, but everyone including Nancy had returned to work the second Quinn arrived. And Quinn didn't just arrive—he strode across the floor like a conquering hero. To make matters worse, all the women were giving him simpering glances when what he needed, in Magenta's opinion, was a short, sharp, shock and someone to stand up to him. Whatever dream state they were both trapped in, this was getting out of hand.

But could this *really* be Quinn? Magenta's head was reeling. Quinn in the sixties was none other than the gorgeous biker, in a jauntily angled Trilby hat and a dark overcoat that, instead of making him look silly, only succeeded in making him look like the master of the sexual universe.

'Magenta,' he said curtly, shrugging the coat off his shoulder and handing it to her along with his hat.

He knew her?

'That's a better look for you,' he said, giving Magenta the most intrusive inspection yet. 'I like to see a woman in a dress with some shape to it.'

What?

'Keep it up,' he said approvingly. 'And remember, I expect the same high standards from my staff at all times—'

'Yes, sir,' she said smartly, playing along, which was all she could do—other than acknowledge Quinn was a beyond the pale chauvinist—as well as the best-looking man she had ever seen in her life. With his tough-guy body clothed in a sharply tailored dark suit and impeccably knotted tie, he looked amazing.

'I'll need you for a meeting later,' he said, as though they had been working together for ever. There was not a shred of equality between them, Magenta registered with a spear of concern.

'So no gossiping with the other girls in the kitchen when you're supposed to be making my coffee,' Quinn warned.

Would that be the coffee with the extra-strong laxative in it? Magenta wondered.

'And absolutely no lunch break for any of you girls. You'll have a lot of work to get through by the time I finish the meeting I'm going into now—understood?'

Actually, no, I'm a bit confused. Magenta thought Quinn had called a meeting to discuss her position with the company going forward, but perhaps that directive hadn't made it through to the sixties. She decided to prompt him, if only to find out how much had travelled with her in the dream. 'So, you're having another meeting first?'

'What are you talking about?' Quinn demanded impatiently.

'Another meeting before *our* meeting…?'

Quinn had no worries about touching Magenta. Taking hold of her shoulder in a firm grip, he steered her into an alcove out of sight of the rest of the office. 'Not in front of everyone, Magenta…' And then his eyes warmed in a way that made her heart stop. 'Later, maybe—if I have the time.'

Magenta's mouth formed a question, but she was so stunned by Quinn's brazenly sexual behaviour her voice refused to function, and when she did speak it was only to ask Quinn what he wanted her to do with his hat and coat.

'Why, hang it up, of course,' he said as if she were one card short of a pack. 'And when you've done that I'll need plenty of coffee—hot, strong and black. Oh, and when you come into the meeting later, don't forget your shorthand notebook.'

'My—?'

'You're the office manager now, Magenta—that's quite a promotion for you. You'll have to sharpen up if you want to set the seal on this position.'

She'd set something in concrete—the deeds of the building, perhaps, before she dropped them from a great height on Quinn's head...

But someone else owned the building now, she remembered, biting her lip. Steele Design had been called Style Design when her father had bought it. She had no stake at all here.

Now she found herself staring at the back of her own office door as Quinn closed it in her face.

Then it flew open again. 'Magenta?' Quinn rapped. 'My office. Now.'

You could have heard a pin drop behind her. They all anticipated her immediate dismissal, Magenta guessed. She countered that expectation with her sweetest smile. 'Of course,' she replied respectfully; respectful was good—essential—at least until she learned the ropes. Walking inside, she shut the door behind her.

'Let's get one thing clear,' Quinn said, handing Magenta the hairpiece she had left on his desk. 'You do not use my office in my absence for grooming purposes. You do not come in here at all, unless at my express invitation. And, if I'm at work early, you are too.'

'And how would I—?'

'How would you know?' he interrupted, narrowing his eyes. 'I was coming to that. Do you have your notebook? No? Carry it with you at all times? You have a "must do" list, don't you? When I give you a memo to alert you to the fact that I will be in here at six in the morning, I expect you to note it down. Why are you late, by the way?'

Magenta opened her mouth and wondered which of the million and one reasons on the tip of her tongue would work best in Wonderland. 'I apologise,' she said, thinking better of making a fight out of it just yet. 'I just thought you might appreciate a couple of days to become acclimatized.'

'Acclimatised? I've come over from the States, not the moon. What's wrong with you limies?'

Limies? *Whoah*; that was an old term Magenta guessed hadn't been used much since the war. The term was a hangover from the way-back-when days, when British sailors were given limes to counteract scurvy. Surely they were way past that?

'I need you here on time, Magenta,' Quinn continued to rap. 'You're my assistant as well as the office manager. If the job's too much for you, just let me know.'

'It isn't—I mean, yes, sir,' Magenta spat out crisply, stopping just shy of a salute.

This was novel. This was annoying and confusing. And, alarmingly, it was pretty amazing too. Quinn was pretty amazing, with all that dark hair escaping his best attempt to tame it from falling over his brow. And those eyes, steely and fierce—not to mention the *body* currently concealed beneath some pretty sharply tailored clothes. Here at last was a man who was really worth taking on. Had she met her match at last? Forget all that nonsense about not wanting to add him to her workload; she would gladly put Quinn on her 'must do' list.

'Please accept my apologies.' She wanted to keep the job, such as it was, didn't she? 'I forgot you intended making such an early start. And I'll be sure to remember my, er, "must do" list in future.'

'Be sure you do. Just remember, this might be your first day on the job, but it gets you no special favours from me. I expect you up to speed by the end of the day. And any thoughts you might have had about taking time off before the holidays, cancel them.'

She had to swallow her pride. She'd been doing a lot of that recently, but it would only be until she found her feet down this complicated rabbit-hole—or, better still, until she woke up. 'I'll get the coffee, shall I?'

'Yes, you do that,' Quinn agreed. 'And take that dead rat with you.'

'Of course.' She was only too happy to drop the horrible hairpiece in the first bin she found.

The men filed in and sat around the boardroom table as Magenta set the coffee down in front of Quinn. Her team, nearly all female, could have run rings around them, she concluded five minutes into the meeting. What were the women doing sitting outside typing? Surely some of them had flair?

She glanced at Quinn as he rubbed a hand across his eyes, as if he had forgotten something. Was it too much to hope he had intended to include some of the women in the meeting?

'I should have asked for coffee for everyone,' he apologised—to the men. 'Magenta?' he added brusquely, shooting an impatient glance her way.

She wasn't going to snap back in front of the men, she decided. Quinn might have lost all sense of business protocol by speaking to her so rudely, but she hadn't. 'No problem at all,' she said pleasantly, sweeping out of the room, surprised by the openly admiring glances she was attracting. She would gladly exchange those looks for a return to the casual acceptance of her gender she was used to. The men's gazes burning a hole into her back made her really uncomfortable, though she was pleasantly surprised when one late arrival rushed to hold the door for her. Were her sensibilities changing too?

No. She bridled outside the room, hearing some very male laughter erupting behind the door. Quinn barked a command and there was silence, but Magenta got the distinct impression that the laughter had been directed at her.

She made the coffee and took it into the men, but held back from serving it. If they wanted a coffee, then one of them would have to pour it. She left the room and returned with her notebook as instructed. She didn't know shorthand, but she could write fast.

And she had to. Quinn wasn't short of ideas, most of which she agreed with, but it would have been nice if he consulted his team along the way, rather than issuing instructions. He ignored her completely. She might have been invisible. 'Can I ask a question?' she said at one point.

'If you want to leave the room, you don't have to be coy,' he said while the men sniggered and Magenta's cheeks flamed red.

'I don't want to leave the room,' she said, conscious of the other men looking on with interest as the little drama unfolded.

'Then please be quiet,' Quinn rapped impatiently. 'Can't you see we're having an important meeting here?'

And clearly it was a meeting she wasn't up to taking part in, according to Quinn, who seemed stuck in a chauvinist mindset.

What to do? She could argue her point, but it would only be counterproductive in this company. She wanted Quinn to listen to her and to take her seriously. She would have to play this subtly for the sake of the team she had already decided she must build—at least until she got the hang of the workings of this strange new world.

But as she sat through the meeting, Magenta's anger grew. As she'd thought, many of the men weren't up to much, while she was increasingly certain that the women currently wasting their talents typing up dictation were being held back. Everything was upside down. She sighed, frustration beating at her brain. She was impotent to do anything about it until she'd worked things out.

'Magenta?'

She jumped with surprise as Quinn rapped out her name.

'If you find it so hard to pay attention, I can always get someone to replace you—'

Quinn wasn't joking. She was in imminent danger of losing her job. And this might be a crazy dream-world, but right now it was all she had got.

CHAPTER SIX

WHEN the meeting ended, Quinn asked Magenta to remain behind, and her heart sank as the last man out of the room threw her a pitying look. But even if this was a dream she had to defend her corner. Was Quinn content with a weak team? Wouldn't he at least evaluate the skills of his female workforce and give them a chance? The more she thought about it, the more fired up she became. 'This is quite an experiment you've got going on,' she commented lightly as she shut the door.

'An experiment? This is no experiment, Magenta. This is my company, and you work by my rules or you walk out that door and you don't come back.'

'You can't just fire me.'

'Watch me.'

Was she *au fait* with sixties employment law? No. And what good would she be to the girls she hoped to recruit if Quinn threw her out?

'For someone so recently promoted, you have a disappointing attitude, Magenta—which is why I want to speak to you.'

'I'm just surprised by the quality of the team you've drawn around you.'

'Firstly, it's not in your remit to pass comment on my decisions. And secondly, that's not my team. That's a batch of individuals I am evaluating.'

Like battery hens. 'Ruthless' didn't even begin to describe Quinn. She was almost sorry for the men.

'I'm evaluating everyone's performance—and I have to tell you that you are my biggest disappointment to date. Instead of being thrilled by your promotion, you seem discontented.'

'That's not the case at all.' Above all she had to hold on to her job. How else would she fight for recognition, not just for herself but for her colleagues? 'I'm overwhelmed by my new role, and your trust in me.' She held back from batting her eyelashes. 'You won't have to wait until close of play today. I'm up to speed now and I promise I won't let you down again.'

Suspicion flared in Quinn's incredible eyes, which she quickly took care of. 'I hope the notes I've taken down are what you require?' She offered them for his approval.

He ignored them. 'I'll let you know when you've typed them up. And one more thing, Magenta.'

'Yes?'

'Your duties include running the office and managing the cleaners, the girls in the typing pool and those on the switch-board. They do not include interfering in my business meetings. Is that clear?'

'Even if I have an idea I'd like to put forward?'

Quinn's expression would have sent grown men scurrying for cover, but Magenta pressed on. 'There are a couple of things I'd like to suggest for the good of the company—and I only mention them as your office manager and secretary to save you unnecessary aggravation in the future.'

'Spit it out.'

'Take smoking.' Quinn was an overwhelming presence in the room—a fact her body refused to ignore however she felt about it. Determinedly, she pressed on. 'Nancy mentioned you have people working here who suffer from asthma, heart conditions.'

'And you think I should get rid of them?'

'No!' Magenta exclaimed, wondering how two people could be so far apart in their thinking. 'I want you to ban smoking in the office.'

Quinn laughed as if she had said the funniest thing that year. 'Tell you what,' he said. 'I'll let you handle that.'

'Okay, I will. It's either that or I'll have to open all the windows wide—and I don't think you would want the girls' work-rate to drop if their fingers seized up with cold. Didn't you say there would be a lot of work coming down the line for them?'

Quinn's face creased in a deceptively attractive smile, but his eyes were dangerous. 'Nicely done, Magenta, though I must admit I prefer my secretaries decorative rather than combative.'

A shiver of worry crept down Magenta's spine when Quinn added brusquely, 'Are we finished here?'

'Yes. Yes, of course we are.'

'You're sure I've heard all your complaints?'

So now he had her down as a moaner. *Great.* 'I'll get started on those notes for you, shall I?' she said brightly.

'You do that,' Quinn said, turning back to his work. 'Oh, and don't forget to take the coffee tray with you when you go.' He didn't even bother to look up from the document he was studying.

'I hope this is satisfactory?' Magenta asked Quinn later that day, handing him the typewritten notes she had prepared. It was a long time since she had typed anything without the option of making corrections on a computer.

'Don't deviate from this standard.' He handed the document back again.

Could she survive this level of praise? She had only spent most of her lunch hour mastering the art of using a cranky typewriter with a ribbon that came off and keys that stuck. From what she'd seen, all the office hardware needed a thorough overhaul. This might be the sixties, but surely they didn't have to use faulty equipment? She put her concerns to Quinn.

'You've just put yourself in charge of repairs and renovations. I hope you can handle that on top of your other new duties?'

She would have to. But she was so eager to get stuck in, she was taking on more and more, when what she really wanted to do was form a team. To call together and convince those girls in the typing pool that they could do a lot more than type up lists and letters for the men.

'Dinner tonight?'

She stared at Quinn. 'Would you like me to book a dinner reservation for you?'

'I'm prepared to make a few allowances until you get up to speed, Magenta, but if you don't start paying attention when I speak to you my patience will very quickly run out.'

Quinn's *patience*? Had she missed something?

'I believe I just asked you if you would care to join me for dinner tonight.'

Her heart raced. Her mind said no. But how could she refuse him without causing offence?

How could she accept Quinn's invitation to dinner without compromising her position? Since falling down this rabbit hole he had shown her no warmth at all—though he had shown the occasional flicker of another type of interest; if her heart would stop hammering long enough for her to say anything remotely intelligent, she must find a way to refuse him. 'I'd love to have dinner with you, but unfortunately I have so much work to do…'

'You have to eat.'

His charm offensive was overwhelming. 'I'll probably have a sandwich here. I'm conscious of the tight deadline you're working to as far as launching the ad campaign in the New

Year is concerned, and I'm also working on some ideas of my own.'

'You're doing what?'

'Trying a new angle.' Her voice was starting to shake. Quinn's expression wasn't exactly encouraging. He couldn't imagine a lowly woman coming up with a single original idea. She owed it to the team she was now determined to build to prove him wrong.

'I take it these ideas you mention have nothing to do with the work you do for me?' His tone was critical.

They had everything to do with the creative work she wanted to do for him. 'Correct, but—'

'If the work you do for me suffers…'

'It won't suffer.'

Standing up, Quinn propped one hip against the desk, managing to look both formidable and desirable at the same time. 'It had better not,' he said.

Half-man, half-beast—all male… The shout line on a sixties massage-cologne rushed into Magenta's mind. The thought of massaging it into Quinn was quickly stifled. She held her breath as he stared at her thoughtfully.

'Let me see those ideas when you're ready.'

Did she have to feel so gratified at his grudging concession?

'And don't tire yourself out working on personal projects to the point where you're no good to me.'

'I'm only too happy to stay behind and work.'

'You should have asked the girls to help you.'

The girls had enough to contend with from the men during normal working hours without Magenta asking them to stay behind and do more work for her. 'I'm fine—honestly. You go.'

'*May* I?' Quinn demanded ironically. 'That's very good of you.'

'I'm sorry—I didn't mean—'

'Goodnight, Miss Steele. Remember to lock the door behind you when you leave.'

Watching Quinn stride towards the exit made her wish that just for once she could be a *femme fatale* that no man could walk out on.

Dream on, Magenta thought wryly, turning back to her work.

She was stiff from sitting at her mean little work-station for hours on end, working on the final tweaks to the campaign, when the sound of the lift arriving made her tense with alarm. She felt exposed and vulnerable without an office door to lock and sat bolt-upright as the lift doors slid open.

It was almost a relief to see Quinn emerge, but what was he doing here?

Her heart thundered with anticipation. 'Have you forgotten something?' She hurried to greet him. However much Quinn infuriated her, there was no doubt he injected life and vitality as well as a sense of security into the empty, silent office— though she still felt uncomfortably like a soldier on parade.

'Miss Steele.' Quinn's eyes were sparkling in a very un-Quinn-like way—which was to say his expression was both warm and amused, leaving her a very confused and shaken-up soldier. 'Can I get you something?' she pressed.

'Coffee?' Quinn suggested.

'No problem.' She could smell the night air on him, cold, clean and fresh. There was snow on his collar, and ice crystals sparkling like diamonds on his thick, black hair. It was a change to see Quinn looking so windswept, a good change that took her back in time—or was that forwards?—to a young biker removing his helmet and shaking out his unruly mop of inky hair.

'You didn't expect me to come back tonight,' Quinn guessed correctly. Shrugging off his overcoat, he tossed it over the back of a chair and walked with her to the kitchen. 'I saw the lights from the street and took pity on you.'

'How kind,' she murmured. 'Strong and hot?' she said, pushing the kitchen door open.

Quinn's laugh was low and sexy. 'If you say so.'

Were they flirting? 'I'm talking about coffee.'

'And so am I,' he assured her. 'Put a dash of this in it.' He produced a bottle of very good whisky. 'You looked worn out earlier, so I thought I should bring you something to get your blood flowing again. Something told me you might baulk if I offered you fortified wine.'

'Whisky is my drink of choice, as it happens. You know me well.'

'I don't know you at all, Miss Steele, but that is something I intend to put right.'

It was a tiny moment of connection between them, and she wanted to protect and nurture it like a candle flame.

Quinn was way ahead of her.

'Apologies in advance for contravening one of your feminist by-laws.'

She gasped as his lips brushed hers. In the same instant, he pressed her back against the kitchen counter and, with one powerful thigh nudging her legs apart, he drew her close. 'Forget the coffee,' he murmured, teasing and nuzzling her neck and mouth in a way that delivered a powerful charge to every sex-starved part of her. 'You need this more.'

Oh yes, she did, Magenta realised as she wound her arms around Quinn's neck. What her sensible side would have to say about it when she woke up in the morning was another matter. But she was dreaming and, according to the law of dreams, anything was possible, even forgetting her inhibitions where sex was concerned. She would just have to put up with Quinn kissing her like a god.

Quinn's hair was thick and lush, his body was hard and strong, and she was instantly aroused. Quinn's heat was iced with night air and the taste of mint was on her tongue. He had splashed on some cologne—musky, spicy, warm and clean— and his stubble was an unaccustomed rasp against her face. He was an expert in the art of seduction who knew just how to tease, stroke and nip, until she was pressing herself against him, writhing, sucking, biting, practically demanding the invasion of his tongue as she showed him in no uncertain terms that she had fully embraced the concept of free love—at least in her dreams.

But somewhere deep inside her a warning bell was ringing, and that bell was determined to spoil everything. It said that she might be on a fast track to pleasure, losing all sense of right and wrong, but Quinn was still firmly in control. She was strong in everything else she did, except this. Free love was one thing but it had to be on her terms. She'd put a price tag on it, Magenta decided, and that price tag might just buy a chance for the team she planned to build.

Using every bit of mental strength she possessed, she pulled back. 'I'll make that coffee for you.' Turning away, she continued to prepare their drinks with hands that shook slightly. 'Do you think you could spare the time to look at the ideas I'm putting together?'

'Would I like to see what you've been doing when I'm paying you to work for me? I think I should, don't you?' Propping his hip against the counter, Quinn waited until she had finished and then he led the way back into the office, where he swung her ideas book around. 'This is good. What gave you the inspiration?'

'Research.' She could hardly say, the benefit of living fifty years from now. 'I'm keen to push the campaign to the next level.' She had never cheated in her life before, never needed to.

'Your idea certainly moves things somewhere,' Quinn agreed dryly. 'Do I take it you weren't impressed with the team you saw in action earlier today?'

'You could say that,' Magenta admitted as Quinn stared at her keenly.

'Maybe they just need time to settle in.'

'There is no time to settle in if you want to launch in the New Year.'

'So you're suggesting I accept a campaign designed by a woman?'

'Is that so crazy?'

'You've forgotten the natural order of things, Magenta. Men lead at work so that women can enjoy a certain lifestyle.'

'Women can do that for themselves, given half a chance.'

'And I don't let them—is that what you're saying?'

'Maybe men feel threatened—'

'Not this man.' Quinn cut across her.

She took her courage in both hands and went for it. 'Then prove it by allowing women to play a part in your campaign.'

His lips curved; he took it well. 'How do I know that there's anyone working for me, other than you, that has this flair?'

'You'll never know until you give everyone an equal chance to prove themselves.'

'If there's so much latent talent here, why has no one put themselves forward before now?'

'Because women want to keep their jobs, so they keep their mouths shut. Is there any reason good enough to make you ignore a possible seam of in-house talent? I think we must consider our female audience when we design a campaign.'

'What do women want?' Quinn didn't even pretend to think about it. 'Who cares when men pay the bills? This is business, Magenta, not some feel-good society for you to float around in. Men earn the money women spend—remember that. So men are our target audience.'

She hated herself for trembling with awareness of Quinn when he was preaching this heresy. But Quinn was a product of his time, Magenta remembered, which made what she had to do while she was a visitor in this dream world all the more important. 'But you've just admitted women do the shopping, so they have control of the finances.'

'Nonsense. Are you the most argumentative woman I've ever met?' he demanded. 'Who tells a woman what to buy, Magenta? Her man.'

'Not this woman.'

Quinn looked at her and almost laughed. He controlled it well, but at least he'd lightened up. That was a small victory of sorts, Magenta supposed, wondering if her heart would reach some critical point where it would have to slow down.

'All I'm asking you to do is to tune in to your audience, Magenta, but sometimes, I think your head's elsewhere—like another century, maybe.'

Close. But she couldn't stop now. 'If you go on with this belief that we only have to sell to one sector of the community, then this company will sink like a stone, taking your investment with it.'

There was silence, and then to Magenta's relief Quinn's face relaxed as another idea occurred to him. 'Why don't you illuminate me on the correct way to reach every member of our target audience?' Challenge turned his steely gaze to fire.

CHAPTER SEVEN

'I'D BE pleased to explain,' Magenta said, facing up to Quinn. She had to look up at him; he towered over her. 'There are plenty of women in the workplace trying to keep a family afloat.'

'You think I don't know that?'

How attractive was that crease in his cheek? And how determined was she not to be distracted by it? 'Women have always been fighters, Quinn—they've had to be—and if you want to know what appeals to them you capture the whole of the market—their men and the next generation, too.'

'And if I want to know how to appeal to women I should ask you?'

Like Quinn didn't appeal to every woman he met. But he didn't face up their ads. 'You could ask any of the women who work here for their opinion. Use the resources you have, don't ignore them. Ask them what they like to buy, to use, to experience.

'You're suggesting we run a series of trials?'

'Why not?'

'Involve women in our brainstorming sessions?'

'Of course.'

'Persuade me.'

Quinn's eyes were dark and smoky; how she longed to. But this was her chance; she couldn't blow it. 'Okay. So, women want to buy your products because they're dependable, exciting and they can trust them—but women want to command attention too. They want to look sharp—they want to be in control.'

'And they want to do all this while they're sitting behind a typewriter knocking three bells out of their expensive manicure?'

'And so the ad has to say to them,' Magenta drove on determinedly, *'You're in charge!'*

'That's a dangerous line to take.'

'Are you telling me men are so fragile they can't survive a challenge from a strong woman?' She held Quinn's gaze. Feeling strong whilst pulsating with lust was confusing, to say the least.

'You're a strong woman, Magenta.'

'Yes, I am.' She knew Quinn was testing her, looking for cracks in her defences. He knew she wanted him to yank her close and devour her with kisses. 'But I'm only one example of a strong woman,' she told him coolly. 'I'm sure there are many others right here in this office.'

'Some men don't find strong women attractive.'

And you, Quinn? Magenta longed to ask him, but she already knew the answer. Quinn was highly sexed—hot, feral, dangerous. Her body was ringing proof of that. Of course he liked strong women. Quinn would like the challenge of subduing them.

'I never discount a woman's needs.'

'If you do, it's your loss.' She had thought he was talking about business, but as Quinn's lips curved she realised he was teasing her and that his mind was on anything but business. It was time to sharpen up that sleep-deprived brain of hers and take this battle to the next level.

'Why don't you get two glasses and we'll have a drink?' Quinn suggested. A sexy grin played around his lips. 'You should take some down-time occasionally.'

Yes, she could go with that—she could let drink fuzz her

mind and make that her excuse for giving the green light to Quinn's white-hot charm offensive—but she wanted more out of life than fleeting satisfaction. 'I'm good. I'd like to finish this work so it's ready for you to see in the morning.' That was the right thing to do. She should remain strong.

She should do a lot of things, Magenta reflected as her body melted like butter when Quinn closed his hands on her arms. Business was one thing, but this was something very different, and she was tired of keeping up a front. She was tired full-stop, and felt dreamy and reckless… And Quinn was…Quinn.

'Better?' he murmured, curving a smile as he dropped a kiss on her mouth.

She sucked in a ragged breath, exclaiming softly somewhere deep in her throat as Quinn deepened the kiss. This was some dream. His hands were lazily coasting down her back while her responses were quickly changing from tentative to hungry and on to greed.

She almost staggered when he stepped back.

He steadied her and then gave her a mocking look.

'Why?' she said, feeling hurt and confusion overwhelm her. She never lost control, except for this one time.

'Because you're tense.'

She got what she deserved. Magenta passed her hand across her lust-swollen lips and then kept it there as if she could hide her arousal. They both liked to be in control, but Quinn was far better at this than she was. She was hardly a practised siren, and even in a dream her skills hadn't improved in that direction.

Quinn moved behind her and she tensed as his warm hands found the tender spot on the nape of her neck where all the stress had collected.

'I told you there was tension,' he said, proving how skilled he was at clearing her mind of anything but sensation.

She didn't argue as he began to massage the stiffness

away. She doubted anyone could move away from that touch. Quinn's breath was warm on the back of her neck and his body was only a breath away. She exhaled unsteadily. Quinn was making it impossible to think. Did he know how powerfully he affected her, how her body yearned for him? She wanted him. She hadn't even thought about her curves before, let alone that they would fit Quinn's hands so well—if only he would touch her.

'Why don't you talk me through your work plan for the rest of the week, Magenta?'

He could switch tracks in an instant, leaving her reeling in his wake. She'd been right to be wary, and now it took several valuable seconds to get her brain in gear. 'I've typed up a work plan which I've left in your office. Shall I get it for you?'

'That won't be necessary.'

Quinn liked this game. He liked playing with her. And from what she'd seen of him so far Quinn only ever played to win. 'I'd like you to see it,' she said, breaking away. 'I want you to know I won't let you down.'

'You won't get the chance. There can be no special favours because you're new to the job, Magenta. I expect the same productivity from you that I expect from the other girls. More, in fact, because I made the decision to put you in charge.'

Which was why she had made sure to be prepared. Going into the office, she retrieved her list and passed it to Quinn, who scanned it briefly before handing it back to her.

'You're going?' She watched Quinn shrug on his overcoat.

'Did you expect me to stay?'

Anger consumed her. Quinn knew just how to work her. She would have to move a lot faster if she were to avoid becoming his puppet—the woman who could not only knock up an excellent coffee on demand, or a spreadsheet or two, but who could also oblige Quinn in more personal areas of his life. What he needed was a strong woman to take him in hand, Magenta concluded. She had always believed she was strong—but was she strong enough?

Quinn's laughing eyes put that challenge directly to her. 'We'll have a lot on tomorrow, Magenta. I'll expect you in the office first thing, and I will make no allowances for the fact that you're working late on your own project.'

'Of course not.' *You unrepentant barbarian*, she thought, smiling pleasantly.

'Sleep well.'

'I will.' *And I wouldn't go to bed with you if you were the last man on earth*, she thought, holding the smile. *Unless you asked me nicely.*

She refused to notice how attractively Quinn's lips pressed down. 'I almost forgot this,' he said.

'What is it?' she said, gazing at the plain-brown paper bag.

'A sandwich. In case you get hungry while you're working.' One last amused glance, and Quinn stepped inside the lift doors.

He knew she wanted him, Magenta realised. He no doubt also knew she was a complete novice where men were concerned. This was shaping up to be one hell of a fight. Whichever world they inhabited, she always liked a challenge.

Fortunately you could still flag down a cab in the sixties. If anything, the streets were calmer and the traffic far less frantic. Even the pavements were in better repair. And for a sixties buff like Magenta even the smallest detail, like a billboard featuring a youthful Elvis Presley in his latest film, was a source of the utmost fascination. But there were some things she couldn't get used to: the lack of central heating in her house, the ice on the inside of the bathroom window, a bed that made her feel like the filling in a particularly well-chilled sandwich.

Tucking herself in beneath a cumbersome sheet, and several thin blankets with a ridiculously small eiderdown perched precariously on top, she realised that her passion for the sixties had made her overlook the privations that had existed then. She had taken the best parts—the comfortable and exciting parts—and had romanticised them to fit in with how she thought the sixties should be. But the truth was somewhat different, as she was rapidly finding out. And now she only had a couple of hours in this frigid room to rest her head before getting up for work again.

The phone rang, annoyingly. Without opening her eyes, she risked one warm arm to reach into the chilly air and pick it up. The voice on the other end of the line was deeply male and instantly recognisable. 'Magenta? Are you awake?'

'Wh…wh…?' How long had she been asleep? Five minutes? Less? 'Yes?' Magenta realised she was sitting bolt-upright and practically saluting.

'Aren't you out of bed yet?'

Quinn's deep, sexy voice lacked all vestige of charm. 'Of course I am,' she huffed, getting tangled up in the phone cord as she rolled out of bed.

'Good, because I'm at the office, and you should be too.'

She stumbled over the cord.

'Magenta, what's happening there?'

'Nothing. Why?' she demanded, untangling herself.

'I can hear a lot of banging about.'

'That would be the front door closing,' she covered for herself, stretching the curly phone-cord to its limit as she peered through the open bathroom door. 'Just getting the milk in.'

Quinn hummed. 'Forget breakfast and get in here, will you? A national newspaper has announced that its first colour supplement will be launched in the New Year, and—'

'And we're going to be in it!' she exclaimed excitedly.

'That's the plan.'

'Fantastic!' It was fantastic. And would be even more so if

Quinn could only bring himself to trust her with the smallest detail, rather than expecting her to type up the minutes of his latest meeting. But first things first; the sooner she got herself back to the office, the sooner she was back in the game. 'I'm just putting the phone down for a second,' she said, knowing the phone cord wouldn't stretch far enough. 'Hang on.'

Rushing into the bathroom, Magenta looked in vain for the shower. She would have to take a quick bath—a cold bath, as it turned out. Too late now to notice the switch on the wall and realise she'd have had to turn it on some hours earlier if she wanted the luxury of hot water.

'Fantastic?' Quinn bellowed as she picked up the phone again. 'Is that all you have to say about it? I can't believe you're awake yet, Magenta. This is a national first and I want a big, visual splash for Style Design in that first supplement— Magenta? Are you still there?'

Barely. She had stepped into the frigid water and made a big splash of her own. Down, up and that would have to do it. Teeth chattering, she reached for a small, scratchy towel.

No fluffy bath-sheet warming gently on a heated towel-rail.

No bath sheet, full-stop.

Lodging the phone between her shoulder and chin, she jumped about to keep warm as she flung open the single wardrobe door. Now here was a thing—a disposable paper dress in a black-and-white op-art pattern. Paper clothes would be put to good use in clinics in the future, though not in this flamboyant design. She smiled wryly. Goodness knew how, but dresses like these were making it to the fashion pages of the sixties, judging by the magazines she'd seen in the office. This particular company's bold claim was that they were not only at the cutting edge of fashion, but were ready to supply disposable clothes for space flight and settlements on future moon-colonies.

How high would Quinn take her?

Thoughts like that definitely belonged in the realms of fantasy, Magenta decided as Quinn uttered a phrase that was bang up-to-date in whichever era he lived.

She settled for a safe wool dress, deciding to keep the outrageous paper mini-dress for the Christmas party. Why shouldn't she break out that one time and surprise Quinn? Tradition demanded everyone let rip during the holiday celebrations, and surely that had been no different in the sixties? And wasn't she incredibly comfortable around paper these days? She would just have to hope Quinn would see the irony in her choice of outfit. But that was for later. The sleek wool dress she chose for now was in an attractive shade of coral and had a wide, form-enhancing belt, which Magenta buckled securely. She looked the part and was determined to work the role fate had given her to the very best of her ability.

What else could she do? she reasoned as she soared upwards in the office lift. At least she'd get to see Quinn again—and, in spite of his manner towards her last night, she felt the customary buzz of anticipation as she walked into the office. She was already looking for him, practically scenting the air like a doe on heat searching for the buck. Yes, Quinn was a bad-boy, but would she seriously want to change her dream lover into a weed?

CHAPTER EIGHT

THIS sixties version of the office where she worked was more like a stark, bare stage than the technology-crammed work setting Magenta was accustomed to, with its anonymous banks of twenty-first century computers and purposefully androgynous personnel. Here in the sixties everyone dressed to impress and showed off their assets to best advantage. Fortunately, she had adapted quickly to her new role as office manager, and found that her natural air of authority even had most of the men begrudgingly following her orders. Not Quinn, of course. The only orders Quinn followed were his own.

'Always liked a strong woman,' one of the men who had teased her earlier declared as she took the cigarette from his hand and stubbed it out.

'No more of that,' Magenta said firmly, realising that, the firmer she was with these men, the more they seemed to like it.

All except for Quinn, who when she did see him chose to ignore the fact that they had spent a large part of the last evening flirting—or verbal jousting, as Magenta preferred to think of it. He repeated his warning—with his lips very close to her ear—that she would pay the consequence if outside interests detracted from her work for him. Quinn had otherwise left her alone with a pile of work she was sure he had added to in order to punish her for oversleeping that morning. Not that her lips cared about that. They were too busy tingling from the memory of his kisses.

The day passed quickly, the only down side being the lack of Quinn. Magenta let Nancy and the rest of the girls leave early again, feeling they had spent another day under the heel of unreasonable men; she was equally determined that all that would change soon. If there was one thing she was determined to do before she woke up again, it was to make a difference for those girls.

Would she wake up if she fell asleep at the office? Magenta wondered, resting her chin on the heel of her hand. After all, she had woken up here at the office. Who knew what might happen in such an upside-down world? She glanced across at the group of men hanging around in the hope of being able to say goodnight to Quinn—and possibly kiss his backside too, Magenta reflected waspishly. It was nothing short of a miracle that women had found the energy to prove themselves in the sixties, in her opinion. And on top of that they were expected to run a home.

So what had changed? Magenta wondered wryly. Things were pretty much the same in the twenty-first century.

Quinn appeared and everyone straightened up. Even Magenta was guilty of trying to give a good impression. There was no harm in looking; Quinn was one good-looking man.

'Still working, Magenta?'

She was surprised when he came over to her rather than heading for the men.

'This is good,' he said, scanning her latest idea.

'And when it's finished you can see it.' She covered her work protectively.

'You should share your ideas,' Quinn told her.

'And I will,' she said. Just as soon as she had organised a team. She was determined to recruit from the typing pool and the switchboard. She had to get those girls believing in themselves so they could leave the corral behind for good.

'When can I see it?' Quinn's gaze sharpened.

'As soon as we're ready.'

'We?' he said suspiciously.

'This type of work is usually undertaken by a team.' As his eyes narrowed she could tell she'd gone too far. 'What I mean to say is, with your approval, I would like to canvas opinion in the typing corral.'

'The typing corral?'

Why was she staring at his lips? 'I mean the women who type,' she said carefully. It wouldn't do to put his back up. Not yet. 'They're closed off from the rest of the office as if they're in a corral.'

'And?' Quinn queried.

'We're losing out on their opinions. I just thought that maybe their thoughts on the various products you're promoting could be useful to you.' She spoke mildly but felt like a tigress defending her cubs.

'Perhaps…' Quinn thumbed his sharp black stubble.

'And I have another idea for you.'

'Why aren't I surprised?'

Was Quinn trying to overwhelm her with that incredible stare? 'I realise I'm only the office manager, but I thought if you would allow me to build a team—in my own time, of course—perhaps we could test our ideas, one team against the other?'

'Men against women?' Quinn looked immeasurably smug, as if the end result were a foregone conclusion. 'You're serious about this?'

'Never more so.' She held Quinn's stare, feeling her body's response to him like a flame of heat that brought her blood to boiling point. But she had to ignore those glorious eyes and focus on her goal. 'I've heard that slots for advertising in the new colour supplement are so sought-after they are going to be decided by a team of style-setters.'

'I've heard that too. We have to be at the top of our game.'

'Which is why I thought if everyone was involved you could cherry-pick the best ideas to produce the final, winning scheme.'

'You don't give up, do you?'

She knew better than to respond to that.

'I hope you don't make me regret this.'

'So you agree?' Holding Quinn's gaze was dangerous, but she was fast becoming an adrenalin junkie.

'If this is a wind-up, Magenta…'

'I promise you, it isn't. I just know that some of those girls are going to want to be involved, and that some of them are bound to be good.'

'You like a challenge,' he said.

'Doesn't everyone?'

'No. Most people like to play it safe, but not you. You seem to thrive on living dangerously—which is good,' he added when she was about to say something, 'because I have plans for you.'

Magenta's heart leapt for all sorts of reasons, any of which she'd settle for.

'I'm going to give you the chance you've asked for. I've got nothing to lose,' Quinn pointed out with a shrug. 'I'm going to give you the running of the year-end party too. That's coming up fast—do you think you can handle the pressure?'

'I'll handle it.' Here in the sixties it was some way to Christmas, so she had plenty of time.

'And don't bring me any old ideas. Think outside the box, Magenta.'

Which was exactly what Magenta and her twenty-first-century counterparts were renowned for. Now she just had to adapt that flair to a different era.

'Well, don't just stand there—go work on your ideas. We'll have another chat in the morning.'

'Yes, sir.'

Magenta was thrilled to think Quinn might let the girls have a chance. But had she taken on too much? She would have to get a credible team together as fast as she could and be ready to present to a judging panel of one.

'Those trials you mentioned?' Quinn said, turning at the door.

'Yes?'

'Warn the girls I'll be looking for their opinion on a selection of new products.'

'I will.' This wasn't a victory—not even close—but it was a great improvement on how she had felt when she'd first fallen down the rabbit hole.

The following morning Magenta put her plan to the girls. She'd fully expected them to look at her as if she were mad. What she couldn't have expected was that they would warm to her ideas quite so quickly. She guessed that had everything to do with her explanation that it would mean going head to head with the men.

'But Quinn has the final word,' Nancy observed. 'How does that work?'

Magenta slipped down from her perch on top of the table in the ladies' room, which was where they had assembled to be sure of being out of earshot of the unfair sex. 'If there's one thing I know about Quinn it's that he's first and foremost a businessman.'

'A warrior with the eyes of a lover,' one of the girls argued, shivering deliciously as the others murmured their agreement.

Why was she so jealous, suddenly? Magenta wondered, quickly smothering that thought. 'He'll certainly fight for the company.' She had to believe that. 'And he wants that contract. You're wrong to be concerned, Nancy. Quinn might be tough, but he's fair.'

She was sticking up for Genghis Khan now! But the girls were agreeing with her, so she'd stick with that line for now.

'Is it going to be a fair fight, or is this just a ploy by Quinn to keep us quiet?' Nancy demanded.

'It's a genuine competition—just as the competition for inclusion in the new journal is genuine. I wouldn't waste your time otherwise. Put a challenge in front of Quinn and he can't resist it—neither can I, neither can you. And I'm as sure as I can be he'll play fair.'

'But would he ever go for our ideas over those of the men?'

'Why not if they're better ideas, Nancy? And what do we have to lose? This is a fight to better our jobs.'

'And smash the men!' Nancy's cheeks were already glowing at the thought.

'Don't forget the pleasure it will give us,' Magenta reminded her.

'When we bury those worker bees?' a girl with sweeping glasses suggested to agreement from her friends. 'We're with you, Magenta.'

'There's just one more thing.'

'Which is?' Nancy said suspiciously.

'We have to do something first to help Quinn, to demonstrate how cooperative we can be.'

'I might have known it,' Nancy exclaimed to a background of groans.

'You might enjoy it,' Magenta said hopefully.

'If it includes typing, cleaning or extra coffee-making duties, I'm out,' Nancy assured her.

'Are the men expected to pre-qualify too?' one of the other girls asked.

'I think we all know the answer to that question,' Magenta admitted. 'But let's concentrate on things we *can* change rather than worrying about those we can't.'

'So, what do we have to do?' Nancy demanded, hands on hips.

'Trial a few products?'

'Oh, that sounds nice,' Nancy said sourly. 'Let me guess— pan scrubs, sweeping brushes and limescale-removal cream?'

'Make-up, beauty products and clothes, actually. And you get to keep the samples.'

'Quinn's buying us,' Nancy observed sceptically as the other girls exclaimed with pleasure.

'No. I believe Quinn genuinely wants our opinions,' Magenta argued. 'It's as simple as that.'

'Nothing is ever as simple as *that*,' Nancy commented, studying her nails.

'Maybe not,' Magenta agreed. 'But are we going to let a few tubes of lipstick stand in our way?'

'No,' the girls shouted, while someone else chipped in. 'This is bigger than lipstick. This is a fight for freedom.'

'To the barricades!' Nancy exclaimed as everyone laughed. 'But don't forget to put your make-up on first.'

'So, are you with us, Nancy?' Magenta asked, turning serious.

'You bet I am. After what I've taken from those men today, I'm itching for a fight.'

She might have known, Magenta thought as she entered the room where they were to trial the products at the head of her girls. Sweet little dressing-tables had been set out for each of them as if they were life-sized Barbie dolls. On top of these was spread an array of high-end beauty products guaranteed to make any woman's heart beat faster. Fortunately, both Magenta and her newly formed team knew how to play it cool—which was just as well, seeing as Quinn's team was standing ready with their clipboards waiting to take down their thoughts.

'How nice,' Magenta murmured, as if trialling nail varnishes and lipsticks was all her candy-floss heart had ever yearned for. She gestured that her team should choose a seat, and the girls smilingly obliged—but then they were in on the surprise Magenta had in store for the men.

Said men could hardly keep the smiles from their smug faces, though Quinn appeared quite relaxed about the trial he'd set up. And gorgeous, Magenta registered, with his crisp, white shirt rolled up to the elbows and beautifully tailored black trousers moulding the shape of his muscular thighs and hips with obscenely loving attention to detail. Undressing such a spectacular specimen would be a privilege...

'Aren't you going to sit down, Magenta?'

'If there were enough chairs.'

'Here, take mine—I won't be needing it,' Quinn explained as he held out a chair for her.

There was a distinct rustle of expectation in the air as the men adopted serious expressions. Once again, they were ready to jeer and jibe at the slightest cue from Quinn, but he remained brooding and unmoved. And now all Magenta had to do was to discover if she was as bold as she had promised the girls she would be on their behalf. Picking up a lipstick, she pursed her lips. 'Glittering Fool's Gold,' she murmured, straightening up again. 'What do you think of it?'

'What do I think of it?' Quinn said, frowning.

'Yes. What do you think of it?' Magenta repeated, standing up. She had everyone's attention now. 'According to men, women do everything for their benefit—so surely your opinion matters more than ours?' She tipped her chin to stare Quinn in the eyes, all the while smiling pleasantly. 'Would you like to taste it?' An audible intake of breath rose around her, but before there could be any misunderstanding she handed the lipstick over to Quinn. 'You don't have to put it on. You could lick it, or suck it.'

Taking her arm, Quinn drew her out of earshot of the others.

'This is a serious trial and you're a disruptive influence. What the hell do you think you're playing at, Magenta?'

'Conducting a serious trial,' Magenta insisted in a heated whisper. 'This lipstick looks as good as the one I use, but it tastes like medicine mixed with pond swill. Would you kiss a girl wearing something like that twice?'

Quinn's eyes narrowed dangerously and it took all her strength to hold his gaze without flinching. The glint in his eye said she'd gone too far again, but he couldn't argue with her motives. 'I'll give you the benefit of the doubt this time,' he said. 'But keep it straight from here on in. No jokes. No *double entendre*. Don't try any more tricks. Understood?'

'Perfectly.'

When the girls had finished testing the make-up, Quinn eased away from the wall. 'Thank you, all of you, for your co-operation. Please take anything you like.'

'Excuse me…?'

'Yes?' Quinn's head shot round when Magenta spoke up.

'We girls didn't want to be passive observers in the trial, and though we've enjoyed the experience enormously we do have some products we'd like you men to trial.' She almost had to shout over the ensuing uproar. 'We thought it could only benefit the campaign to get some insight into male products too, to cover all the market,' she said quickly, seeing Quinn's expression turn thunderous. He had granted her one favour and now she was stretching his patience to the limit, while the men were baying for her blood. After all, what could a woman possibly know about a man's world?

Quinn silenced the roar of protest.

She had to risk everything on one final throw of the dice. 'I wouldn't have thought of it,' Magenta said innocently. 'I have you to thank, Quinn, for pointing out that our advertising efforts are largely directed at men. As this is the case, the girls and I thought it only prudent to be sure we're on the right track by trialling some of the new male products and getting your thoughts on them.'

'Yes, yes, yes,' Quinn interrupted impatiently as the other men around him started to complain. 'Magenta's right,' he added to her amazement. 'I said we'd have a fair trial, and we will, which means the results cannot be assessed until we have views from both ends of the spectrum.'

With men at the top end of that spectrum and women no-where, presumably, Magenta thought. But this wasn't the time to be greedy—not while everything was going to plan. 'Would you give us a minute to set up?' she asked before Quinn had a chance to change his mind.

'Take all the time you need. More than a minute and I'm out of here. What's this?' Quinn demanded when Magenta returned at the head of her team.

'A shaving chair I borrowed from the local barber.'

Quinn shook his head in cynical surprise, but insisted on lifting it out of her hands all the same. 'Where would you like it?'

'In the centre of the room, please.' The men weren't smirking any longer, Magenta noticed. 'All we need now is a volunteer. What, no one? Won't anyone help us with our trial?'

Someone sniggered.

'I will.'

All eyes were on Quinn, who was already loosening his tie.

CHAPTER NINE

'THANK you, Quinn.' She only had to hold his gaze to realise it contained all sorts of messages that made her yearn inside, most of which were, thankfully, indecipherable to anyone else in the room.

Everyone held a collective breath as Magenta helped Quinn take off his jacket. She could feel his warmth through the cool of his cotton shirt and an array of muscles flexing beneath her fingers. The spread of his shoulders was a challenge in itself, and though she wasn't small she had to stand on tiptoes to slide his jacket off them. She gave it to one of the girls to hang up.

'Would you like me to take my shirt off too?' Quinn suggested.

'That won't be necessary, thank you.' He really knew how to make her heart thunder. 'If you would care to sit down…?'

Quinn arranged himself on the leather seat, and before she lowered it she secured a protective cover around his neck. Then, tipping him back so she could reach the sink, she stood over him. Their stares connected. Lying flat on his back, Quinn's was amused, while hers could only have shown how much she was enjoying this moment of domination. To have Quinn's strong, tanned face beneath her fingers and his gaze, laced with irony, daring her to do her worst was the best challenge she could have dreamed of. 'Would you be more comfortable with your shoes off?'

'I'll keep them on, thank you—I might want to make a quick getaway.'

Quinn's comment lifted the atmosphere at a stroke and even Magenta laughed.

'Get on with it,' he warned. 'Remember, I want all those reports on my desk before lunchtime today. In fact, everyone,' he said swivelling round in the chair, 'you can go now. There's no need to hang around while Magenta conducts her trial. I'll file my own report.'

And if that didn't cause comment in the office, nothing ever would.

'Would you have preferred an audience?' Quinn demanded as their colleagues filed out.

'It doesn't matter to me either way.' She would carry through with this whatever happened, though a few-dozen chaperones would have been nice. And safer.

'So? Where do we begin?' Quinn demanded.

'With a warm towel to soften your bristles before I shave you.'

'You'll be using a safety razor, I presume?'

'Would you prefer I used a cutthroat?'

Quinn laughed. Magenta doubted anything qualified as 'safe' if Quinn had anything to do with it. The thought of touching him, let alone massaging him with her inexperienced fingers, was a mountain she had to climb without a safety rope in sight. 'There's just one thing.'

'Which is?'

'You won't—'

'I won't what?' Quinn demanded.

'You won't try to kiss me?' Magenta blurted awkwardly.

'You don't want me to?'

'I don't want any surprises—I don't want my hand to shake, or I might cut you.'

'You really know how to charm a man, don't you?'

No. That was one thing that was completely outside her area of expertise.

'I don't plan to surprise you, Magenta.'

'Good.'

'I don't plan to kiss you either.'

Bad.

'Are you ready?' Quinn demanded. 'I don't have all day.'

The damp towel had been warmed in the prescribed manner and she took the greatest pleasure in winding it tightly around Quinn's face.

'It helps if I can breathe!' he exclaimed, rearranging it.

'Sorry.' And now she had a dilemma, Magenta realised as she rummaged through the products. Should she choose the *Head Man* toiletries, for the man who was a man's man from nine to five and a lady's man after six? Well, Quinn was hardly a nine-to-five man, and so far there had been no sign of any ladies.

So, how about men who wore *English Leather* or nothing at all?

Magenta's appreciative gaze swept down Quinn's muscular form. She mustn't even think that way.

How about something called *Inferno*? The shout line was enough to put her off: *if she doesn't give it to you, get it for yourself.* Cologne seemed a poor substitute for the type of gift that ad was hinting at.

'Well, have you chosen a product range to trial on me yet?' Quinn demanded impatiently.

'Yes, I have, actually. Something called *Forbidden Fruit*.'

'Sounds reasonable.'

'"The Lime of Least Resistance".'

Quinn's lips tugged and Magenta could hardly keep her face straight. The sixties ad lines were really corny. If she couldn't come up with something better, it was time to get out of the business—though, of course, her knowledge of the future should give her team a head start.

Was that cheating? Not really; it was just good business sense, Magenta reasoned. 'Ready?' she asked Quinn.

'As I'll ever be,' he told her dryly.

Soaping Quinn was fun, shaving him less so, but only because he put her on edge and she was genuinely frightened of cutting him. And, far from being softened by the hot towel, his stubble remained just as dense and sharp as it had been when she started the process. Plus, she had to lean in very close, which made her even more aware of him, especially when each time she pulled back it was to find Quinn's disturbing stare levelled on her face. He had the most beautiful face—strong, clean lines and a healthy complexion. And those lips…

She had never been so intimate with a man before and felt her whole body respond as her hands adopted a new, caressing touch as she positioned Quinn on the padded head-rest. She couldn't help her breasts brushing his arm as she worked and the feel of Quinn beneath her hands was intoxicating. She had to concentrate very hard indeed on this trial.

'Not bad,' he admitted, testing his chin when she'd finished. 'I might keep you on.'

'You should be so lucky.' She laughed nervously, only now realising how tense she had become.

'Don't forget the massage—that's my favourite part,' Quinn insisted. 'And I can hardly be expected to give my verdict on the products until I've sampled all of them.'

'Of course.'

'Warm the cream in your hands first.'

The air stilled between them as she picked up the container and poured a little of the cream onto her hands. She warmed it between her palms as Quinn had suggested, and the sliding sound of cream on skin was yet another reminder that she was batting well out of her league.

'Don't be shy,' Quinn advised her dryly.

'I'm not shy.' She started tentatively at first and then grew bolder. She closed her eyes, allowing her fingers to map the shape of Quinn's face. She wanted to imprint every detail on her mind so she could remember this moment whatever happened next. Quinn's brow, his ears, his neck, his lips—nothing was forbidden to her and she indulged herself to the full.

It was Quinn who brought the session to an end. Operating the lever at the side of his chair, he sat up. 'I always suspected you were a dark horse.'

'Did I do something wrong?'

'On the contrary, that was the most sensuous massage I have ever experienced.'

'But what about the product?'

'What about the product?'

'You're supposed to be assessing it.'

'I thought I just had. Write it up,' he said, removing the protective sheet from his neck and handing it to her. 'Give yourself full credit. I'll expect your report on my desk by lunchtime today, Magenta.'

'And you'll listen to the ideas of my team now?' She held her breath.

'I gave you my word, didn't I?'

She wanted to leap up and kiss him, but of course she had more sense.

'Anyone stand out for you?' Quinn demanded on his way out of the door.

So many of the girls had flair she hardly knew where to begin. 'Nancy, Maria, Josie—' *Oh, to hell with it.* 'If you could just give them all a chance.'

'And?' Quinn said, suspecting there was something more.

'Equal pay with the men?'

'You don't want much,' he said wryly.

No, but while he was in a good mood she was going to ask for it.

'All of these things have to be earned,' Quinn observed. 'Regardless of gender.'

'So you'd consider making changes?'

'When I do, you'll be the first to hear.'

'Thank you.'

'Don't thank me—you'll be typing up the memos. If you can't take the heat, you'd better get out of the kitchen, Magenta.'

'I can take it.' Yes. *Yes*! Oh boy, could she take it. This was an incredible turnaround from the most intransigent of men.

'Good, because you'll be adding all this new work to your regular duties.'

Would there come a point where she crumpled beneath the pressure? Well, if there did, Quinn wouldn't care—so she had better not. Getting that break for the girls was the only thing that mattered.

Magenta could barely wait for Quinn to leave the room before flinging the protective sheet he'd handed her into the air with a whoop of excitement. The next step would be planning a new ad campaign with her team.

The girls were giddy with excitement just at the thought of being taken seriously. The sexism and chauvinism in the office knew no bounds and Magenta could hardly believe that such intelligent and vital individuals had been disregarded solely on the basis of gender. How could these women have been kept down for so long, subjugated by the men? How could any manager afford to waste such a valuable resource?

Having assured her new colleagues that their ideas really were going to be listened to, she got down to writing up her report and delivered it to Quinn before lunchtime as instructed. To her amazement, he handed her a typewritten sheet. 'My report,' he said.

'Thank you...' Perhaps they were getting somewhere after

all. Holding the sheet of folded paper close, she left the room feeling warm inside. And, yes, even a little triumphant. If all the battles ahead of her would be so easily won…

'Leave my door open, will you?' Quinn called after her.

'Of course.'

Quinn wasn't so bad, Magenta decided, settling down at her desk. He just needed handling. She was in charge of collating the results for the trials and, now she had Quinn's report, she could make a start.

Studying the sheet of paper he'd given her, Magenta's eyes widened.

Dinner tonight, Quinn had written. *Pick you up at your place at eight—no excuses.*

It was less of an invitation and more of an instruction.

Magenta tensed. Reports forgotten, she stared into space. Kisses were one thing, but anything more… She had just experienced a prolonged sensory experience with Quinn and now he was calling her bluff. Was she up to a one-on-one meeting after work?

'Did you want to talk business tonight?' She turned with the note in her hand to speak to him through the open door.

'What else?' Quinn said impatiently, waving her away.

A business meeting. Well, that was all right, and would give her a chance to learn more about Quinn. She felt a thrill of anticipation. Of course she could handle it. She was a big girl, wasn't she? She could always say no. How could she turn Quinn down without offending him? That might put the girls' future prospects in jeopardy, which she would never do.

Turning in her chair, she flashed Quinn a faint smile and a nod. It didn't do to look too eager.

Hemlines were getting shorter, according to the fashion magazines the girls kept around the office. Venturing into one of the tiny boutiques, that had sprung up down a street Magenta knew would one day be turned into office blocks, was a temptation she couldn't resist. Armed with cash from her wage packet, she was ready to shop. The chance to wear one of the daring outfits for Quinn being showcased in the shop windows was slightly less appealing—she'd feel safer in a sack—but she guessed he might baulk at that for their evening out.

Swinging London was the first headline she noticed on a news stand as she walked along, together with a picture of the Beatles. She definitely had to make some sort of effort to be stylish. Dragging her gaze away, she saw a hairdressing salon and decided to make that her first stop.

A stylish young man with floppy hair and tight, flared trousers arranged Magenta's long hair so that it hung loose down her back and was dressed fairly high at the top. Taking it up at the sides, he gave her a fringe so long it caught on her eyelashes.

Realising she could buy make-up at the salon, she chose some smoky eye-shadow, passing on the pale foundation with the option of white lips. She had to contend with the lady behind the counter giving her some strange looks as she battled with the unfamiliar pre-decimal currency. She finally managed to get it right and handed over what seemed to her like a very small amount of money before leaving the shop.

Now she had to hunt for an outfit to wear that evening. She had fun trying on all the vintage clothes and realising they were new. There was nothing subtle about sexiness in the sixties; she already knew that. Though she didn't want Quinn to think her a frump, a couple of inches above the knee was as far as she was prepared to go. Rejecting a cobwebby, crotcheted dress, she chose a high-necked, soft turquoise silk with trumpet sleeves that flattered her figure without exposing too much of it.

'You could go bra-less,' the shop assistant informed her. 'You've got the figure for it.'

What and show off her nipples? Give Quinn a handy

barometer to go by? He hardly needed that sort of encouragement. 'I'd prefer to wear a bra.'

'What about this no-bra bra?' the assistant suggested. 'It's almost sheer, but it does offer some protection...' She weighed Magenta up. 'If that's what you want.'

'It is pretty,' Magenta agreed and she definitely wanted all the protection she could get.

'You could try these hip-huggers to go with it. Or some matching bikini-pants in the same flesh-coloured lace?'

'They're very flimsy.'

'That's the idea.'

'I'll take them.' She just wanted to get out of the shop now. The girl's close scrutiny was beginning to make her feel uncomfortable.

'Which one?' The girl was holding up a pair of knickers in each hand.

'Both.'

'You're sure they're not too flimsy for you? I do have some heavy-gauge serge in the back.'

Was it so obvious that Magenta's twenty-first-century lifestyle meant her choice of underwear depended on what washed well on a short cycle and lasted longest?

CHAPTER TEN

MAGENTA braved her freezing bathroom to take a bath and then dressed carefully. When the doorbell rang, her heart went crazy. If this was a dream she was certainly taking her time waking up, she thought as she hurried downstairs.

And now she didn't want to wake up. Quinn looked amazing. Standing on her doorstep wearing a heavy overcoat over his suit, and with a long, silk scarf slung casually around his neck, he was unreasonably handsome—like a hero stepping out of a dream. In full sixties hero-about-town rig, he really was something else.

'Ready to go?'

'I am,' she confirmed, trying not to notice the silver-grey Aston Martin DB5 parked behind Quinn on the road. She'd half expected to see a motorbike parked at the kerb.

It didn't do to mix up dreams with reality, Magenta resolved, still gazing at Quinn's fabulous car. 'I can't believe it's in such immaculate condition,' she murmured, hardly realising she was speaking out loud.

Quinn looked at her curiously. 'Do you mean the car? Why wouldn't it be?'

Of course, it must be brand new; she had almost betrayed herself. 'I love it. You're a very lucky man.'

'And the harder I work the luckier I get,' Quinn said dryly. 'Have you forgotten something, Magenta?' he added. 'Your earrings?'

It wasn't as if *she* felt naked without earrings, but as she touched her earlobes Magenta remembered that no self-respecting sixties woman would be seen without them—whether they were colossal hoops or feathers trimmed with bells, not to mention the all-important chandelier for the woman who considered herself a cut above the rest. 'I'll be right back,' she said. 'Come in out of the cold while you wait. Close the door.' She flung this over her shoulder as she raced upstairs.

Neat pearl-drops in place, she returned to the hallway.

'Perfect,' Quinn approved, looking her up and down.

His assessment was a bit intrusive for a business meeting, Magenta thought, but she'd let it pass. Quinn escorted her to the car and, opening the door for her, saw her settled inside.

'Where are we going?' she asked with interest as he took control of the high-powered machine.

'I haven't decided yet. What kind of food do you like?'

'Anything, pretty much.' She was curious to see if Antonio's was open. The restaurant was situated in this direction and was one she knew. Antonio's was famous for injecting the serious up-market restaurant quarter in London with Italian sunshine and some much-needed *joie de vivre*. It had been in the same family since the late fifties, being one of the first to bring spectacular ice cream and the art of curling spaghetti around a fork to London. So it should be a bustling concern in the sixties, Magenta reasoned, peering expectantly out of the window. 'But this isn't the way to Antonio's,' she said with concern as Quinn took a turning that led to a leafy and exclusive London suburb.

'Antonio's?'

'Sorry, I was just thinking about an Italian restaurant I used to go to round here. So…' She tried for light, and predictably ended up with an anxious wobble in her voice. 'Have you decided where you're taking me yet?'

'I thought I'd show you my etchings. *Joke*,' Quinn said

dryly when he heard Magenta's sharp intake of breath. 'I thought we'd go to my house.'

'Your house?' Her mouth dried. 'Should I be worried?'

'Do you want to be?' Quinn threw her a glance.

'Of course not,' she said, crossing her legs.

'Good—but reserve judgement. Remember, you haven't tasted my food yet.'

'You're going to cook for me?'

'Is that a problem?'

'No.' *Just a surprise*. Genghis Khan in a pinny was quite a thought.

What was she getting into? Magenta wondered as Quinn swung into the drive of a grand, porticoed house. Was this where he usually brought his business associates for a chat? She'd had him down as a very private man who would never mix business with his private life.

She tried not to act like Quinn's country cousin as he showed her round his house. Magenta's father lived in some style, but nothing close to this. The music room on the first floor, with its full-sized harp and selection of valuable period instruments, was like something out of a palace. Quinn was a connoisseur as well as a warrior in business. The thought of how that combination might translate in the bedroom made her senses roar. When Quinn slipped her coat from her shoulders and his fingers brushed her neck, she betrayed herself by shivering.

'Are you cold?'

She stared into Quinn's amused gaze. They both knew the opposite was the case. Why was she feeling so embarrassed and unsure of herself? Sexual attraction between a man and a woman wasn't unheard of, was it? Whatever their respective positions in life and whatever the era.

To the sex-starved it was. She moved a sensible distance away from him.

Shrugging off his overcoat, Quinn left her for a moment

and when he returned it was with two glasses of amber liquid that glowed seductively in the cleverly designed lighting.

'What is it?' Magenta said as Quinn handed her the glass.

'Single malt.'

She laughed and lightened up. 'You remembered. Do you know many women who drink whisky, Quinn?'

'Does it matter?'

'Not at all—I just wondered if you liked non-conformists.'

'You're not a non-conformist, Magenta.'

'How can you tell?'

'Because non-conformists all look the same.'

'Like hippies?'

'Exactly.'

Now they were laughing together, and against the odds she was beginning to relax in Quinn's company. She really liked him—too much. She couldn't afford to let her guard down and expect to survive the experience unscathed.

'Shall we get down to business?' she suggested, putting her glass on the table.

Quinn's lips pressed down with amusement as he put his glass next to hers. 'I'm ready if you are.'

This was business?

Quinn dragged her into his arms and his kisses were a brushing, teasing, honeyed reminder. 'I shouldn't...'

'You should. You must.'

Quinn's dark eyes glinted with humour and then he deepened the kiss. The chance to experience everything she had ever dreamed about with Quinn—a man who exuded power, raw and unrepentant—was now a very real possibility. She had always been awkward with men before, concerned she'd get it wrong, but the way Quinn was kissing her, binding every part of her to him, left very little to chance.

Best of all, Magenta reasoned, nothing could go wrong in a dream—there were no consequences. She was free of inhibition and embarrassment. Her twenty-first-century world of metro-males and smooth-cheeked mummy's boys had never seemed further away as Quinn persuaded her this was one sixties experience she shouldn't miss out on.

Now his tongue was teasing her lips apart, leaving her in no doubt as he plundered her mouth what he would like to do to her and how very good he'd be at doing it…

She exclaimed with shock when he pulled away.

'Do I frighten you?'

'*You* frighten *me*?' The awkward laugh was back again; she was more frightened of her own feelings than Quinn.

Quinn hummed. 'You play it tough,' he said. 'But I'm not so sure.'

'You mentioned supper?' She was out of her depth and sinking fast. Quinn was compelling, and had drawn her to him like a magnet, but his insight had left her feeling exposed and vulnerable. For all she knew, Quinn had caveman morals wrapped in an Ivy League veneer. He certainly promised pleasure with no price to pay, but life was always more complicated than that. Was it possible dreams were more straightforward?

'Omelette good for you?'

Quinn had changed into jeans and a shirt, which made him look dangerously user-friendly as he led the way into his kitchen. 'Yes. Perfect, thank you.'

She found it bizarre that they were talking about food while she was still shimmering from the effect of Quinn's kisses.

Quinn appeared unaffected. 'Cheese? Plain? Herbs? That's the selection I have on offer tonight.'

She inhaled swiftly when he levelled a keen gaze on her face. 'Cheese would be good.' Why must she always feel as if Quinn knew everything she was thinking? Did she need to be so sensitive? Quinn was a hot-blooded man and it was she who was out of sync here. She wasn't embracing the sixties vibe; free love, free from commitment, was the norm.

'Would you like your omelette well done, or a little soft and liquid inside?'

She swallowed convulsively. Must that deep, sexy voice make everything sound like an invitation? 'Moist and not too well-done, please.'

Would she disappoint in the sexual-performance stakes? Quinn was highly sexed, while she wasn't exactly a well-oiled machine. In fact, she was probably starting out at a lower point than a virgin—she knew what to expect and how badly she could disappoint.

'Are you frightened of all men or just me, Magenta?'

'I'm not frightened of anyone,' she protested. 'If I was frightened of you, I wouldn't be here.'

'But you don't think much of men, do you?' Quinn observed as he reached inside the cupboard for a bowl and a whisk.

'That depends on the man in question.'

'Tell you what we're going to do.' He swung around to face her. 'I'm going to make supper, and while I do that we'll talk through your plans for the Christmas party and anything else connected to the business. Then I'm going to make love to you. Does that sound reasonable?'

Her intake of breath was swift and noisy. 'You are one arrogant son of a bitch.'

'Guilty as charged,' Quinn acknowledged calmly.

'I'll eat, we'll talk business and then I'm going home.'

'Whatever you like.'

Couldn't he show a bit more disappointment? She was more mixed up than the egg was about to be, Magenta felt as Quinn reached inside his large and very stylish refrigerator. It must have come over from America with him; this was a time when many people still stored their perishables in a meat safe in the cellar. 'What?' she said defensively when he started to laugh.

'You're as bad as me, Magenta Steele.'

No one was that bad, Magenta mused, taking in the hard-muscled package that was Gray Quinn. 'Explain.'

'You do nothing by chance.' Reaching inside a drawer, he found a pan and tossed it, catching it niftily by the handle. 'You plan carefully and you do your homework. You've proved yourself to be an effective team leader in a short space of time. You know where to locate the rich veins of business and how to mine them. You're wasted behind a desk, Magenta.'

'You've noticed,' she said dryly.

'I notice everything,' Quinn assured her, breaking eggs in a bowl. 'I brought you here because I know you'll be good for the business and I want to talk to you about that.'

She should be pleased. But female vanity, however fragile—and, boy, was hers fragile—demanded more. But Quinn wasn't going to give her anything more. Sex and business was for him the perfect combination—with an omelette on the side.

'Your team will sit in on the next board meeting. If there is an untapped resource in-house, I'm going to use it.'

She struck while the iron was hot. 'So you're going to take down the partition?' she enquired. When Quinn gave her a warning glance, she added, 'As you said yourself, sharing ideas in an ad agency is paramount.'

'Anything else?'

Magenta listed everything she thought might give the girls an even playing-field at work—including banning sexist comments.

'You are turning into quite a force to be reckoned with.'

His thoughts on that were unreadable. Would he crush her, or would he give Magenta and her team a chance?

Quinn pushed a bowl of salad towards her with the instruction to add dressing and give it a toss. She did as he asked and then sat down across the polished-steel breakfast bar from him.

Quinn's gaze remained steady on her face. 'You sure don't go for gentle change.'

'Gentle might not be enough.'

'You want things fast and now.'

Intensity had drawn their heads closer to the point where she could see the flecks of amber fire in Quinn's eyes. It was warning enough, and she started to draw back, but Quinn caught hold of her wrist, stopping her. 'Don't back off now, Magenta.' His voice dropped low. 'You know there's nothing more you love than a challenge.'

Just when she thought she was safe, Quinn reminded her there was another tension between them, and one that had nothing to do with business. Part of her longed to go along with this, to soften and invite as Quinn expected her to. Fortunately, that part was firmly under control.

'You're blushing,' Quinn observed.

Yes, because he had no inhibitions and she had plenty.

The breath hitched in her throat when Quinn ran one firm fingertip very slowly down her heated cheek until it came to rest on the swell of her bottom lip. 'Why are you blushing, Magenta?'

'No reason,' she said, pulling back. 'The heat of the kitchen, probably. I'm impressed you can cook,' she added, moving out of range.

'The men you know don't get hungry?'

'I don't know many men.'

'I taught myself how to cook.'

'That's good.'

'More like necessity.'

She relaxed a little. 'I didn't mean to offend you. It's just, you don't look the type.'

'To cook? What type of man doesn't like to eat, Magenta?'

'Most men have someone to cook for them.' *Yes, even in the twenty-first century*, Magenta thought wryly.

'More fool them. I'd rather trust my own abilities.'

Than those of some woman—was that what Quinn had left unsaid? How much leeway would he give her, or any woman in his business? 'I'm sure you have all the skills required,' she said recklessly.

How was she supposed to concentrate on her concerns at work now when Quinn's eyes had darkened to smoky black?

CHAPTER ELEVEN

SHE was operating on two levels, Magenta realised as she watched Quinn's skilful hands at play on the second omelette. Whether the cautious part of her approved or not, she was violently aroused. And this was the best chance she was ever going to get to discuss business with Quinn, that sensible side reminded her.

'Sit. Eat,' he said, putting a perfectly prepared golden omelette on the table in front of her.

The aroma alone was enough to make her salivate. 'This is delicious,' she said, forking up a feather-light morsel of buttery, golden egg.

Quinn joined her at the table and dumped some salad on both their plates. 'Tell me more about your ideas.'

He never wasted a moment; she liked that about him. It encouraged her to confide more. Quinn was an attentive listener. He asked her about the Christmas party. She took him through her plans as far as she'd got. 'I'm pleased you trust me to take care of it.'

'If I can't trust you on any level, Magenta, you'd better let me know now.'

And there it was again—the change in Quinn from charming host to uncompromising employer in the blink of an eye. She would have to be more circumspect in future, Magenta warned herself.

'I just make these stipulations for the party,' Quinn continued. 'No clichés. No glitz. No threadbare traditions. And, of course, no unnecessary expense. And I love surprises,' he added, having wiped out most of her plan in a matter of seconds. 'Eat,' he insisted.

No one had said this was going to be easy.

'That was delicious,' Magenta told Quinn as she helped him to clear up.

He nodded briefly. 'Let's get on to your talents, your ideas.'

'I work in a team.'

'But it's your brain I want to mine. Whoever came up with those ideas, it was your drive and initiative that brought them to my attention.'

'I can't claim all the credit.'

'Why not?'

'Because that's just not the way we do things.'

'Do things where?'

Ah. That was a little harder to answer.

Quinn shook his head. 'If you want to get ahead you'll have to toughen up, Magenta—unless you want to be stuck outside my door for ever.'

'I don't want to be there any more than the girls want to be stuck in the typing pool.'

Quinn's eyes narrowed. 'Don't push me, Magenta.'

'You make me sound like the most exasperating woman you ever met.'

'By far.'

Now they were both smiling.

Feeling Quinn's heat shimmering on her senses, she glanced at her wristwatch. 'I'm not sure it's sensible for me to be alone with you here late at night.'

'You think you're in danger?'

'I think you could charm the pants off anyone.'

'What colour are they?'

'What?'

'Your pants. If I'm going to charm them off you, it would be useful to know what colour they are.' Quinn's lips curved wickedly.

Magenta's cheeks fired red, remembering her flimsy, flesh-coloured almost-pants. They wouldn't take much thinking away—one tug and they'd be off.

'Why, Magenta Steele, I do believe you're blushing again,' Quinn murmured as he brushed a strand of hair back from her brow.

'It's hot in this kitchen,' she said stubbornly.

'Oh no,' Quinn disagreed. 'I don't think it's that.'

His mouth was just a whisper away. 'Coffee?' she suggested weakly. Pressing her hands on the surface in front of her, she forced herself to push away from him. Glancing round the kitchen, she hurried to collect cups, coffee and spoons.

'Here, let me make it before you scald yourself.' Quinn covered her trembling hands with his.

'Are you trying to persuade me to stay?'

'I don't need to go to those lengths.'

'You're very sure of yourself.'

'Yes, I am,' Quinn agreed.

The breath caught in her throat as he drew her close. Her back was to the table and Quinn's firm thigh was between her legs. She was so aroused, his lightest touch was all it took to make her tremble with awareness. 'I should go.'

'No, lady, you should come.'

As Quinn moved against her, she groaned deep down in her throat. What was the use of pretending she didn't want this? Quinn's touch was firm and sure, and he gave her the kisses she was aching for, stoking the hunger inside her until she was moving urgently against him in the hunt for more contact, more pressure, more sensation. The aching need grew inside her until it dominated her thoughts and occupied her womb where she longed for Quinn to fill her. He had woken a slumbering appetite and it was clamouring to be fed.

'I want you,' she gasped, winding her fingers through his hair so she could pin him to her. Thrusting her body into his, she relished the sensation of his steel against her silk, his muscle against her softly yielding flesh. She was greedy for his lips and rubbed her cheek against his, loving the rasp of his cruel black stubble against her tender skin.

'Not here. Not now,' he said huskily, lifting her.

'Where are you taking me?' Though she was sure she knew. Not in the kitchen, not the first time. The first time was far too special for that.

When Quinn dipped his head and kissed her again, the question became redundant. He took her mouth with a breath-stealing lack of urgency as if he had all night to tease and arouse her. 'Do you remember what I promised you?' he murmured.

That he would make love to her? She would hardly forget a thing like that. She might have had her hang-ups back in the real world, but here in the sixties her body ached for Quinn all the more, knowing his plan. 'Just promise me one thing.'

'I promise to pleasure you until you fall asleep exhausted in my arms.'

One final thud of anxiety beat in her heart at the thought of disappointing him, but she pushed it aside. 'I want something else.'

'Greedy.' Running the palm of his hand lightly over her hair, he continued stroking her, from cheek to neck, before brushing the swell of her breast and the imperative thrust of her nipple with a tantalisingly light touch.

'Whatever happens between us,' Magenta whispered, trying to catch her breath, 'you won't let it interfere with your plans for the business—the chance you've given the girls?'

'They mean a lot to you, don't they?' Quinn murmured against her hair.

'Loyalty means everything to me.'

'Aren't you concerned about your own position in the company?'

'Of course I am, and if I fall short in any way I would expect you to ask me to leave. But not because of this—not because of us.'

'Us?'

Quinn's lips curved. Who knew what he was thinking? The only thing she could be sure about was the way she felt about Quinn.

He gave a dry laugh. 'Do you really think I'm going to mark you out of ten and take that score forward from the bedroom to the office? Your job's safe, Magenta; the company needs you. And, whatever happens between us, I'd be a fool not to consider what your colleagues have to offer. Reassured?' Quinn demanded. 'You should relax more and worry less.'

That might be possible if she had any useful experience in the bedroom department. 'I won't be any good.'

'You're going to be *very* good,' Quinn argued. 'I'm going to make sure of it.'

Quinn's lips were firm and tempting and the expression in his eyes reassured her. She wanted everything he had to give her, starting with tenderness, Magenta decided as Quinn nuzzled her neck. No—starting with fun, she amended when he pulled back to smile his sexy, curving smile. No. That was wrong too. She wanted to feel safe like this, to feel the strength of a man as he lifted her in his arms.

Oh, to hell with it—she wanted sex with a man who knew what he was doing, Magenta conceded as Quinn carried her up the stairs.

Quinn's bedroom was huge, warm and cosy, and was both neat and scrupulously clean. The scent of sandalwood hung in the air and the decor was tasteful—shades of cream, honey and chocolate—the perfect frame for Quinn, who kissed her firmly, skilfully, deeply. He lowered her onto linen sheets without pausing one instant. 'Where did you learn to kiss like that?' she demanded, smiling as she marvelled at his strength combined with such subtlety.

'They produce some great self-help manuals these days.'

This was some dream, Magenta thought, laughing with him; she was going to enjoy every minute if it. Reaching up, she started on Quinn's buttons. Pushing the shirt from his shoulders, she paused a moment to drink him in and wonder what she had done to deserve a dream like this. Quinn's torso was lightly tanned and heavily muscled. He was magnificent—perfect. If she could bottle this dream and sell it on the open market, she could save her company back in the real world without any help from anyone.

'You're so beautiful.' And she was so greedy for him. She tugged Quinn's shirt from his waistband to feast her eyes on his belly, banded with muscle. All men should be like this, and if women ruled the world they would be.

Kicking off his shoes, Quinn joined her on the bed. Stretching out his length against her, he ran his fingers lightly down her arms.

Could anything else feel this good? But when Quinn dipped his head to kiss her she pressed her hands against his chest and made him wait. 'Not yet. I want to look at you; I want to touch you—explore you.' She was finding strength she'd never known she had and, luckily for her, Quinn was willing to indulge her.

She smiled as he tucked his arms behind his head. Inhibitions? Quinn had none. And if Magenta was ever to lose her own hang-ups it was here with this man, and it was now.

She knelt over him, brushing his naked chest with her hair. 'Stay where you are,' she commanded softly when he made to move. Trailing her fingers across his chest, and down over that hard band of muscle to the waistband of his jeans, she teased Quinn as he had teased her. Hearing his shuddering breaths aroused her even more.

'And now it's my turn.'

She gasped as Quinn swung her beneath him.

'Trust me,' he said, seeing her apprehension.

The bond between them was growing, Magenta realised, and she did trust him. She groaned as Quinn caressed her. He was so intuitive; his hands knew everything about her body and sensation was already throbbing between her thighs.

'Is this your first time?'

She turned her face away from him. 'No.'

'Convince me,' Quinn demanded.

'I am worried.'

'About what?' he said. Cupping her chin, he made her look at him.

'I might have healed up...'

He laughed; they both laughed.

'You're frightened I might hurt you?'

I'm more frightened of the way you make me feel, Magenta thought. 'Not that—but I am frightened of losing control. I'm frightened of the sensation that builds inside me each time you touch me. I'm frightened of falling over the edge and never coming back. I'm frightened of experiencing something I can't begin to cope with.'

'Can you be more specific?'

'This is going to sound so stupid to you.'

'Try me,' Quinn suggested wryly.

'I have never—' She swallowed and started again in a firmer voice. 'I have never...'

'Had an orgasm?' Quinn supplied, making her blush.

Her face was on fire. She couldn't speak.

'And you want me to show you?'

'I'm not sure I do,' Magenta admitted.

'Only because you don't know what to expect. When you do, you won't want to stop.'

Her body responded with outrageous enthusiasm to Quinn's proposition.

He took his time undressing her, smoothing his hands down her body while she responded eagerly to his touch. Her desire was reflected in Quinn's eyes. She wanted everything he had to give—more sensation, more caresses—but she suspected Quinn would make her wait now he knew her secret. He would draw this out, allowing her time to think about the magnitude of the pleasure to come—pleasure he would bring her.

He proved this theory now. The more she tried to hurry him, the more his lazy smile assured her that he would set the pace.

'Why?' she demanded finally on a shaking breath. 'Why are you making me wait like this?'

'Because it will be worth waiting for.'

'I've waited long enough.'

Quinn's words and his stern expression, the note of command in his voice, all drove her to the pinnacle of lust—which he knew only too well. Quinn understood everything about her needs. He knew how to make her hungry for him and was shameless about using that power. Cupping her breast, he chafed her nipple through the flimsy fabric of her bra while his hot mouth attended to her other nipple. Her new lacy underwear concealed nothing; she could see that her nipples were no longer modestly pink, but were livid and erect. Her cobweb-fine briefs did even less to conceal the brazen swelling of a body that had to know Quinn's touch—and soon.

He had slipped a pillow beneath her buttocks and now she realised why. He wanted her to see the pleasure he was bringing her—he wanted her to have clear sight of all her erotic zones responding to him as he coaxed them into pleasure.

'I think you like that,' he observed when she sucked in a noisy breath.

'I don't like you teasing me,' she complained, writhing

beneath him as she tried in vain to capture some elusive pressure from his hands. 'How can you do this? How can you wait like this?' She arced towards him, but Quinn was too fast for her, and had already moved his hands away.

'I can't bear it!'

'Well, I can—and you are going to learn the benefit of delay.'

She reached for his belt.

'I refuse to rush.'

'You must—you have to help me,' she insisted. It was then that Quinn pressed his lips to her ear.

'When you're swollen and ready to the point where you can't hold on, then I'll help you.' Lifting her, he deftly removed her bra and tossed it aside. She moved to cover herself, but Quinn wouldn't let her. 'It's my turn to look at *you*,' he said.

She loved the note of command in his voice and, resting back on the pillow, she raised her arms above her head, displaying her body for his approval. Her breasts were full; Quinn approved, she gathered, as he caressed them. When he had suckled to his heart's content, he buried his face in them. 'You were made to be loved, Magenta Steele.'

By you. Only by you. 'Has anyone ever told you you're very good at this?' she said, easing her head on the pillow to look down at him.

'How would you like me to answer that?' Quinn demanded softly, staring at her with amusement.

'With the truth?'

But Quinn just laughed and moved farther down the bed.

She cried out softly, feeling his hot breath on her thighs. 'Oh *please*,' she begged as his strong, white teeth teased and tormented, sharp against her hot flesh. Arcing her body, she made it easier for him to remove the scrap of lace, which was all that was left between them, and then whimpered when he pressed her to him flesh to flesh. She should feel embarrassed—awkward, apprehensive—but instead she was lifting her hips for him. She was ready, more than ready, for the pleasure Quinn had promised her.

And then he touched her.

CHAPTER TWELVE

SHE went quite still. She didn't want to breathe or move in case she did anything to distract Quinn and make the pleasure stop. Time was suspended as he began to touch her in a more purposeful manner. His movements were leisurely so she had a chance to relish each studied movement. Delicately parting her swollen lips, he touched her with his tongue. Rough tongue, hot flesh, warm breath and the steady but dependable rhythm he set up soon brought her to the edge. 'Lie still,' he commanded. 'Let me do everything. Do you understand?'

She could only gasp something unintelligible in reply. She wanted to keep her focus on Quinn and the pleasure he was bringing her.

He began again.

'Oh, no, no, no!' she exclaimed, thrashing her head about on the pillows when he stopped. 'You can't stop now. Even you couldn't be so cruel!'

'Cruel?' Quinn demanded softly, moving back up the bed. 'I'm not cruel. You have no idea how considerate I can be—especially when you follow my instructions to the letter.'

'You are so bad,' she breathed. 'But I will. I will…'

The last thing she saw was Quinn's lips curving and then he was moving down the bed to start again.

'I can't hold on,' she wailed as the tidal wave rushed towards her.

Quinn might have answered; she wouldn't have known. She

bucked convulsively as the first climactic throb of pleasure claimed her, and only heard herself crying out his name when the violent surges of pleasure began to subside. Quinn held her as she writhed beneath his firm touch until she quietened. 'That was…amazing.'

'More?' he suggested.

'I have to undress you.'

'You have to?' Quinn curbed a grin.

'Absolutely. Now I know what I've been missing. Like you said, I have plans.'

Sitting up in bed with her long, dark hair tumbling over her shoulders, she started on Quinn's belt. She hated the thickness of the leather and the stubbornness of the tine. His erection thrust imperatively against the denim, tantalising her, taunting her, and when she finally released the zip it flew back under enormous pressure. 'Lift your hips.' Her voice sounded harsh and primitive, matching the hunger inside her. Inhibitions meant nothing to her now. She was claiming her mate.

Boxers followed Quinn's jeans to the floor, and only now did she hesitate. Quinn might have prepared her to the point of no return, but seeing him naked like this for the first time startled her. Could she possibly take him inside her? He was so much bigger than she had imagined, more brazenly masculine in every way, and utterly unselfconscious about it. Powerful and virile, this was a man in peak condition, muscular and tanned, and right now he was formidably aroused.

'Is something wrong?' he said.

'I want you.' She held his gaze, and Quinn knew from her expression that at this point she needed him to take over.

Reaching out, he brushed the hair back from her face. She felt awkward momentarily, even surprised that Quinn would make sliding on a condom part of the love play between them.

'Can I?' she said shyly.

She had everything to learn and now was her chance. Covering her hand with his, Quinn guided her.

She had always thought it would be embarrassing to manage the mechanics of love-making but nothing was awkward with Quinn. He was so open about everything it made her feel the same way. And this opportunity to explore him, to feel him beneath her hands, warm, hard, veined and smooth, thick and pulsating...

Closing her eyes, she relished the simple pleasure of touch, but then Quinn brought her down to the bed and she was soon distracted. Their kisses grew in heat until they were tumbling over each other as if no touch or kiss, no tangling of limbs or wild, raw, heated embrace, could ever be enough for them. Quinn's body was a passport to pleasure and hers was his to use as he pleased.

But right at the moment, when she should have been at her most receptive, the doubts swept back in. Sensing the change in her, Quinn stilled immediately.

She moved away.

'Are you still afraid I might hurt you?' Bringing her back into his arms, Quinn dropped kisses on her brow, on her eyes and on her lips.

'I'm more frightened of disappointing you.'

Quinn smiled his reassurance against her mouth. 'You could never disappoint me. But if you don't want this...'

'I definitely want it.'

'And I definitely want it. So it seems to me we're riding the same wave here.'

Quinn's lips pressed down attractively as he cupped her face, caressing her cheeks with his thumb pads. From there his hands continued to soothe as his kisses migrated down her neck to her breasts, and from there to her belly and the inside of her thighs. He moved lower, kissing her ankles as he massaged her feet until she thought she would faint with pleasure, before moving on to caress her calves and lick the back of her knees—a place she could never have imagined held such potential for sensation. 'Don't you dare stop,' she ordered him huskily, linking her hands behind her head as he rested her legs on his shoulders. 'Do I please you?'

'What do you think?' Quinn murmured.

She sighed and pressed against him, pressed against his mouth. She didn't want to hold anything back. She wanted to experience everything Quinn wanted to give her to the full. And after he'd brought her to the edge again he straightened up to brush himself against her. He teased her with the delicious foretaste of the pleasure to come until she cried out in complaint. His answer to this was to tease her again, drawing himself more slowly this time over each moist and swollen part of her, until she was relaxed enough for him to stretch her with just the tip.

The sensation was so extreme, so good, that when Quinn made to withdraw this time she thrust her hips towards him, claiming him.

The breath shot out of Magenta's lungs in a rush. She wasn't even sure if she could take all of him; sensing her shock, Quinn worked some magic with his fingers and, with that and his kisses to distract her, he took control. It was only moments until he inhabited her completely.

Quinn moved and she moved with him, marvelling at the lack of pain, the lack of fear, even though he was stretching her beyond anything she would have imagined possible. He filled her in the most pleasing way, massaging her most effectively, and it wasn't long before she was working frantically with him towards the inevitable conclusion. Digging her fingers into his buttocks, she pressed her hips down until she was certain that no part of them was left unconnected, and moments later the first spasm hit her. Crying Quinn's name, she abandoned herself to pleasure, bucking uncontrollably yet registering somewhere in the depths of her mind that her first orgasm with Quinn had just been utterly eclipsed.

It took ages for her to recover and ages for the delicious little aftershocks of extreme pleasure to subside. Quinn rested deep inside her, waiting until he judged her sufficiently recovered, and then he began to move. Rolling his hips slowly from side to side, he brought the hunger back again and the next climax hit her before she even knew it was building. Screaming out his name, she thrust her hips convulsively while Quinn held her firmly in place, making sure she enjoyed every moment of it.

'You're spoiling me,' she managed groggily as he moved to take her again.

'We're only getting started,' Quinn assured her. 'I'm taking the edge off your hunger.'

'Taking the edge off!' Magenta laughed, but Quinn confirmed his intentions, dropping kisses on her swollen lips. 'And when I've done that,' he said, 'just as I promised I would, I'm going to make love to you.'

'Haven't we been doing that?'

Quinn's laugh was low and sexy. 'Come on, Magenta,' he murmured in her ear. 'We both know that neither of us is cut out for a diet of canapés.'

As Quinn was already moving deep inside her she had no intention of arguing with that. Holding her secure in his arms, Quinn was rocking her. 'Harder,' she begged him greedily. 'Take me faster, Quinn.' Then speech was no longer possible. 'Hold me!' she cried out in the last few ecstatic moments.

Cupping her buttocks firmly, Quinn kept her in position as she thrust her fists against his chest. She needed something to brace herself against as her mind was ripped from her body and flung into a world of unimaginable colour and sensation. She explored it to the full, knowing that when she finally quietened Quinn would be waiting to soothe her with reassurances that she was safe.

This was definitely the way forward, Magenta decided, practically purring with contentment as she woke slowly the following morning, thankfully still in the sixties, in Quinn's huge bed. They had made love through the night and only dawn had interrupted them. At the first faint glimmer of light, Quinn had sprung up and left her side.

Her heart filled when he returned from taking a shower. It was no use pretending this was anything casual. She couldn't get enough of him—and no wonder. With a towel slung around his hips like a loin cloth, Quinn was quite a sight to wake up to in the morning. He was the full package, she reflected contentedly, easing her sated limbs. Quinn had the body of a gladiator and a mind like a steel trap. He was funny and tender, and had an appetite for sex that knew no bounds. He was *the* dream lover.

She could so easily make a habit of this, Magenta mused as he strolled towards the bed, drying his wayward hair on a towel.

'It's time to get up.'

'Already?' she complained.

'Work?' Quinn reminded her.

'Work?' she echoed without any of her usual enthusiasm. 'Can't we stay here a little longer?' For the first time in her life, there was something a lot more important than work—such as being with Quinn. Gazing up into his face, she only found it disappointingly resolute.

'Work,' he confirmed, turning on his heels. 'Take a shower; there's plenty of hot water.'

Take a shower—alone? Mageneta frowned, wishing she hadn't heard the distant note in Quinn's voice. After last night she had expected things to be very different between them.

She waited until she was sure he was busy dressing before creeping out of bed. Grabbing her discarded clothes, she held them in front of her. She felt self-conscious suddenly. Quinn made her feel as if she had overstayed her welcome—a sense that only grew when he asked if she wanted a lift to the office.

If? He hadn't even turned to look at her yet.

'I don't want to be late,' he explained. Stepping inside his open-plan dressing room, he started the process of selecting a tie. 'I've got a lot on this morning.'

She mustn't think the worst of him. 'You've called a meeting of the team?' she guessed hopefully.

'Yes, I have,' he confirmed.

If this was an opportunity to get those girls out of the typing pool, she'd forgive him anything. 'Great. I'll be as quick as I can,' she promised, springing out of bed.

She had to be positive about this, Magenta told herself firmly as she stepped into a proper shower beneath steaming spray. She might have known that even in the sixties Quinn would enjoy state-of-the-art plumbing. She had to put her personal feelings to one side and recognise the meeting Quinn had called for the victory it was. And what had she imagined—that Quinn intended to progress their relationship? It was time to get real, time to come to grips with the era in which she found herself, however much that hurt.

But as they drove to the office, and she stared out of Quinn's car window at the sixties cityscape of concrete and high-rise grey boxes, there was nothing she wanted more than a return to real time, real relationships, and an end to this confusing dream if that was what it was. She had expected to be intrigued by everything she saw. She had also expected to be set free to enjoy a whole new set of rules. What she had not expected was those rules leading her to feel so deeply about Quinn, or to find that sexual freedom came with quite such a heavy price tag.

Quinn remained aloof and unspeaking throughout the journey, while Magenta tried to persuade herself that he was mentally preparing himself for the day ahead. Whatever had happened between them, she was determined to show a bright face at the office. There was enough uncertainty there without her adding to it, and the most important thing she had to do today was to tell the girls the good news.

Magenta felt even more positive when she entered the office to discover that the partition around the typing pool had been removed; Quinn had kept his word. Even if the girls were still sitting in rows typing, at least they could see what was going on around them now. And, most importantly, they felt good about the changes, judging by the smiling faces that greeted her.

Her feelings of elation grew when Quinn invited her and the girls to join his team in the boardroom that morning. She had suspected he might, and had briefed the girls beforehand, urging them to speak out and ignore any slights the men might throw their way. 'We have to be professional, even if they aren't,' she'd warned. 'If we want Quinn to involve us in the campaign, it's crucial that we keep emotion out of it. We have nothing to prove in there other than the fact that our ideas are better than theirs.'

'You bet they are,' Nancy had agreed. 'We're behind you all the way, Magenta.'

One of the girls still made coffee for everyone, Magenta noticed. But she told herself she mustn't be greedy. Quinn was right in that lasting change took time to implement. One small step at a time would suit her, so long as that step was in the right direction.

She led the way into the boardroom and acknowledged Quinn as if they hadn't spent the night in each other's arms.

'Magenta,' he greeted her in much the same way. 'Would you and your team like to sit down?'

'Thank you.'

Ever the gentleman, Quinn remained standing until he and his team had seen all the women comfortably settled around the table. Quinn had clearly briefed his team in advance, as Magenta had, and she took this as a good sign. Quinn had also recognised that nothing could be achieved in an atmosphere of taunts and sneering remarks.

'Would you care to begin?' he said. His eyes reflected nothing more than professional interest.

She had to ignore the ache of disappointment inside her and do her job. 'Nancy?' she prompted. 'Would you like to begin by explaining what we have here on the easels?'

Magenta had never wanted to hog the limelight, and couldn't help but be thrilled by the audible gasp of surprise from the men when Nancy revealed the team's first idea. Vivid, graphic imagery and clever text was a winning combination—no one could deny it, not even the men around the table. The general theme was irony, suggesting men must be catered for and even spoiled a little so that women were free to do their own thing.

'You're suggesting we should be pampered and cosseted so we work harder and stay out of your way?' one of the men queried, glancing at Quinn—who had remained carefully neutral up to now—to see his reaction.

'With more women in the work place year on year, I'm sure that's a message that resonates with everyone,' Magenta said, defending her team's premise good-humouredly.

'I think we can see that Magenta's group is coming up with some sound ideas,' Quinn observed. 'Not all of them will fly,' he added, 'but I'm sure we can tailor them to suit our purposes. They will enrich the project—and we shouldn't close our minds to a new approach,' he added when there were murmurs of discontent from the men around the table.

What did Quinn mean? Magenta wondered. She didn't want to rain on her team's parade—the women were all excited that at last they were being taken seriously—but having their ideas 'tailored' to fit in with those of the men didn't sound like the end result Magenta had been aiming for.

CHAPTER THIRTEEN

MAGENTA'S worst fears were soon confirmed.

'Jackson, you take the graphics and work on them,' Quinn instructed. 'And Michael, you handle the fashion side of things. You're more in touch with your feminine side than the rest of us.'

As if a dam had burst, the tension between the men at the table relaxed and they all burst out laughing; it wasn't kind laughter. It was laughter directed at the women in their midst, as if to be a woman was somehow contrary to the laws of business.

Or at least business under Quinn, Magenta thought, feeling betrayed. She could only watch in impotent horror as one by one the ideas her team had worked so hard on were handed over to a member of Quinn's team to progress. The good of the business had to be her only concern if everyone was going to keep their job, but how was she going to explain this to the women who had trusted her? She could feel their shock as well as their disappointment. They would become resigned soon and she couldn't wait around for that to happen. 'May I have a word with you—in private?' she asked Quinn when he brought the meeting to a close.

'About business?'

'What else?' Her gaze drilled into him, telling him in pretty blunt language what she thought of both his question and his manner.

'Won't you sit down?' he said when the last man had left the room.

'I prefer to remain standing, thank you.'

'As you wish.'

Getting up from his chair, Quinn went to stand beside the window, staring out. It had started snowing, Magenta noticed, but that was nothing to the sheet of ice that had closed around her heart. 'I thought we had an agreement.'

Quinn turned to face her. 'And as far as I'm aware,' he said, 'I have fulfilled my obligation to you.'

'I don't understand what you're doing,' Magenta admitted.

'It's clear enough to me.'

'Well, not to me. My ideas and those of my team—I thought you were prepared to consider them, to incorporate them. I never imagined for one moment that you, of all people, would steal them.'

'Steal them?' Quinn demanded. 'What are you suggesting?' His eyes turned black.

Her job, her future—everything hung in the balance, Magenta realized. But this was a battle that had to be fought. 'You took ideas the women have been working hard to perfect and handed them over to the men when all the hard work has been done. I wouldn't mind, but those men don't have an original idea between them. Why should they claim credit for work that isn't theirs?'

'We all work for the same company.'

'Well, of course we do,' Magenta agreed, trying to remain calm. 'But why do you trust the men here more than the women? What makes you assume they have more ability? Quinn, I don't know what's happened to you!' she exclaimed finally, as exasperation got the better of her.

The expression in Quinn's eyes gave her no hope at all.

'Don't ever make the mistake of thinking that what happens between us in our off-duty moments is a green light in the office.'

'I haven't,' Magenta protested. 'I wouldn't—'

'But that's exactly what you're doing,' Quinn cut in. 'Since last night, you have had expectations that go far beyond the bedroom. Well?' he demanded harshly. 'Don't you, Magenta?'

'I thought I could trust you, yes.'

'You can trust me. You can trust me to keep a consistent line. You can't walk in here hours after your promotion and think you can order this business to your liking. New systems have to be tried and proven first. I don't operate a business on a whim—not even my own whim, and especially not yours.'

As each hammer blow landed on her heart, Magenta wished one of them would be violent enough to wake her up. How could anyone share what she'd shared with Quinn last night and feel nothing? How could he switch off from her like this? And, as for the green light, the only light she was aware of was flashing in her brain, telling her she'd made a fool of herself. And their 'off-duty moments'? Quinn made their love-making sound like a useful alternative to counting sheep.

She'd let her team down, and wouldn't make things right by handing in her resignation. And, even if she waited for this nightmare to pass, what if it didn't pass? What if this was her life now?

She had to stay and fight. It didn't matter whether this was a dream or her reality now, her internal dial would remain tuned to the same setting it was always on, which was survival and the determination to defend those she cared about.

She couldn't have felt worse when she called the girls together. 'You're far more supportive than I deserve,' she told them, feeling dreadful when she noticed the small bunch of flowers someone had arranged in a vase on her desk. 'I've let you down, misled you. I can't apologise enough for what happened at the meeting. I had no idea Quinn would take that line. I really thought he was going to involve all of you in the steering group for the campaign. But this isn't the end,' she promised. 'I won't allow your ideas to be squandered or diluted by anyone—and we're not going to sulk or cause a problem,' she added decisively. 'We're going to win this battle by being the very best we can and by selling direct to the customer.'

'Quinn,' Nancy supplied.

'Yes, that's right, Nancy—Quinn,' Magenta agreed. 'Quinn is the only person we have to convince.' She exclaimed with shock as a familiar hand took hold of her arm and firmly moved her aside.

'I was trying to warn you,' Nancy explained discreetly as Quinn went into his office and shut the door.

Could the girls hear her heart hammering? Magenta hoped not. It was crucial that they still believed in her or those typing-pool partitions would soon be up again. 'I'm going in to see him now, to convince him he's made a mistake and needs us on board. I had a word with him after the meeting, but I was too angry to think straight, and so of course Quinn took advantage.'

'That's not such a bad thing, is it?' Nancy said, injecting some much-needed humour into the tense mix. 'We've all seen the way Quinn looks at you.' Nancy glanced around the other girls for confirmation.

'Please stop.' This was absolutely the last thing Magenta wanted to hear. 'I can assure you there is nothing going on between Quinn and me.' Not any longer there wasn't—nor was there ever likely to be again. 'We're as different as two people could be.'

'We all saw the way he touched you just now,' Nancy argued. 'And you never know when a hand on your arm leads to a night on your back,' she added, which made the other girls laugh.

Magenta blushed furiously as the girls continued to tease her, but she was glad they were laughing again. 'Quinn's probably watching us,' she warned. 'We'd better get back to work. We don't want to give him any reason for complaint. Just pick up where you left off,' she said, exchanging meaningful looks with the girls. 'We're not going to give up on this.'

Playing by Quinn's rules, Magenta took him his morning coffee and remained calm as she shut the door. But the moment he looked up at her all her protective instincts for the girls rose up and poured out. 'You've made a mistake cutting the girls out of the equation.'

'Well, thank you for your opinion, Magenta, but I've made the right decision—and you've just proved it.'

'What do you mean?'

'There's no place for emotion at the office, and if I encourage women to seek promotion it would open the floodgates.'

'To feelings?' Whatever she said now would influence every woman's future at the company. 'Isn't that exactly why my team's ideas are more likely to connect with the public than yours? Or do you really think the market deserves another macho ad-campaign dreamed up by men?'

'There's nothing wrong with passion.'

'But no to emotion? How does that work, Quinn?'

'Magenta.' He sighed. 'I have work to do.'

'Allow the girls to work on their projects without consulting the men at every turn and they'll work faster,' she pleaded with him. 'Let them do that, and then you judge which campaign you prefer. Or is that too big a risk for your male ego to take?'

There was a glint in Quinn's eyes as he leaned back to stare at her.

'This is all about you running a successful business, isn't it?' Magenta continued. 'Or did I miss something? And there is one question I would like you to answer.'

'Which is?' Quinn's eyes turned hard.

'What difference does gender make to a successful team?'

He relaxed, making her wonder if Quinn had expected her to attack him on the personal front. 'That's for you to prove and for all of us to find out,' he said.

'We still get our chance?' She kept the pressure on. She had no intention of walking away from this and making things easy for him.

'Don't push me, Magenta.'

'So, that's a yes?'

'That's a maybe,' he corrected her.

She counted it as a victory—however small—and, knowing she'd pushed things as far as she could, she turned to the subject of the end-of-year party. How many more of these cold-blooded meetings with Quinn could she take? It was better to get through as much as she could now, Magenta reasoned.

Quinn was looking at her as if assessing how much she could take on. 'It will be held at the end of this week, well before Christmas,' he said. 'Not much time for you to arrange things, but that suits my schedule better. Well? Don't you have work to do?'

Magenta's head was reeling with all the things she had to do. Quinn had just brought the party forward with no warning at all. She could throw up her hands and admit defeat, or...

'If you can't handle it,' he said, 'just let me know.'

'I can handle it,' she assured him.

'Do you have a theme?'

Did she have a theme?

'If it's good enough, it might buy your team a second hearing.'

In that case, she definitely had the theme. 'I've got the theme.'

Well, she would have in a minute.

'I'm listening.'

'The theme is…' She had to come up with something mildly original or go to the bottom of the class, risking the girls' opportunity to advance in the business in the process. 'Back to the future,' she said as inspiration struck. Okay, it was not so original, but Quinn wouldn't know that. 'It can be interpreted any way people like—but, as we've had the first man in space, and the race is on to land a man on the moon…' Ideas were tumbling over each other in her brain.

'Could be different,' Quinn admitted.

'Could be fun.'

'Could be.'

'I'm interested to see how you interpret it. And Magenta?'

'So…?'

She turned at the door.

'I'm going to trial some of your ideas.'

'You are?' All her personal battles with Quinn were put on hold. She felt like hugging him. Fortunately, after what had happened, she had more sense.

'Tell your team to get back to work on the ad campaign right away.'

'They never *stopped* working on it,' she said quietly.

CHAPTER FOURTEEN

'WHAT are you complaining about?' Magenta heard one of the men, who she'd heard others address as John, taunting Nancy in the main office as she closed Quinn's door. 'You've still got a job, haven't you?'

The men hadn't waited long to resume their bullying tactics, Magenta reflected angrily. It was vital the girls won this battle or there would always be conflict between the sexes in the office. But at least Quinn had agreed to give them a chance. She had even persuaded him to let them use the old boardroom as their temporary campaign-headquarters, and she'd planned to call an emergency meeting there now. But overhearing the exchange between Nancy and their male colleague reminded Magenta how far they had to go—that and the fact that she could wake up at any moment, leaving her new team in the lurch.

'It's tradition,' John was saying. 'You women are supposed to make all the homey, holiday preparations. Just because you have a few letters to type, that's no excuse. We need our mince pies and treats while we handle the real work around here.'

If any useful work was going to get done, they all had to calm down. 'I'm afraid the girls won't be free to run errands for you,' Magenta explained, shooting a warning glance at Nancy.

'Oh?' John demanded. Glancing at his cronies, he sat back, staring at Magenta as if he were a headmaster forced to deal with a child he considered very much his intellectual inferior.

'We're all going to be busy, because we're all back in the race,' Magenta explained. 'Quinn is going to judge both campaigns and choose the one he prefers.'

'But we've got all your ideas,' John said with a laugh in his voice as he traded smug glances with his friends.

'It's what you do with what you've got that makes the difference,' Magenta argued, stealing a glance at Quinn through the office window. 'Girls, follow me to our new headquarters.'

They worked until the end of the day on finessing their campaign, and then the girls insisted on staying behind to help Magenta plan the Christmas party.

'Quinn had a few stipulations to make. Beyond that, we're free to interpret the theme any way we choose.'

'Within a tight budget?' Nancy guessed shrewdly.

'This is hardly the best time to go overboard,' Magenta agreed. 'But I'm happy to cover any shortfall.' Though quite how far her office manager's wage packet would stretch...

'Am I right in thinking you have come up with an idea?' Nancy prompted.

'I have,' Magenta confirmed, revealing her theme for the party.

'But no space-food,' Nancy insisted. 'The only thing I'm prepared to drink through a straw is a cocktail.'

'You don't have to follow a space theme at all,' Magenta explained. 'All I'm suggesting is that each of us interprets the future as we see it.'

'No long hair, caftans, beads or beards!' Nancy exclaimed with relief.

'Not if you remember to shave,' one her friends added with a laugh.

'But the food stays how we like it,' another member of the team insisted. 'All the usual, with my favourite, cheese-and-pineapple on sticks. I'll even volunteer to cover the cabbage with foil.'

'Hang on,' Magenta protested. 'I'm good with cheese and pineapple, but since when do we eat cabbage at a party unless it's in a bowl of coleslaw?'

'We don't eat it,' Tess said, giving Magenta a sideways look. 'We cover the cabbage in foil and stab sticks loaded with the cheese and pineapple into it. Surely you've seen a finished hedgehog before?'

'A hedgehog?'

'Oh, never mind. You'd better handle the cocktails.'

'My pleasure,' Magenta agreed, mentally wiping her brow. Her knowledge of sixties food-fads was non-existent.

'It's just a pity the men are going to be there,' Nancy observed as the girls started working out who was going to be involved in dressing the office and who would arrange the music.

'I'm glad they'll be there,' Magenta argued. 'I want this year's party to bring everyone together. We need something to stop this silly bickering. We have to land this colour-magazine job, and to do that we have to work as one.'

'That'll be the day,' Nancy snorted.

'Well, at least let's give it a try.'

'I suppose there could be worse things than spending the night with a crowd of randy ad men,' Nancy agreed thoughtfully.

'Can we put sex to one side for a minute and concentrate on planning?' Magenta suggested.

'If we put sex aside for as long as that, it will all be over.'

'Give those poor men a chance, Nancy!' Magenta exclaimed, choking back a laugh.

She caught Quinn glancing at them through the window as he walked past. Their eyes might only have clashed briefly, but it was enough to tell Magenta that there was still a live spark between them. Interesting. According to some market research she'd been working on, fifty-nine per cent of men rated women who stood up to them as having the ideal qualities they looked for in a mate. Excellent. *En garde*, Gray Quinn…

Tamping down the rush of heat inside her, she called the meeting to order. 'Can we get back to work, please? There's very little time to do this and we have the campaign to work on during the day—which, by the way, is more important. We're going to give those men a real run for their money when we submit our final ideas to Quinn.'

'And we're going to have the best Christmas party ever,' Nancy added.

Magenta smiled back. 'This is one party that is definitely going down in history.'

How she missed the computer! She never thought she'd say that, Magenta realised, checking the mock-up of the party invitation she had designed. But finally the invitation was ready to go to the printer's and the Back To The Future party was on its way.

'Still here?' Quinn commented, peering round the door.

I could say the same about you, Magenta thought. They were both workaholics.

As Quinn came into the room, her skin began to tingle with anticipation. It was no use pretending she could somehow make herself immune to Quinn. There was a connection between them and she wasn't prepared to let go of it yet. The air had changed—she had changed. She was like an animal scenting her mate. Every breath she took was drenched in Quinn's energy and his clean, distinctive scent. All the more reason to get out of here, her inner alarm advised her. 'I was just leaving, actually.'

'Can I buy you a drink?'

Was he joking? 'It's been a long day.' She kept her back turned so Quinn couldn't see her cheeks flushing with the memory of humiliation. His idea of free love wasn't hers. She was better off without him.

'Are you sure?'

'I'm quite sure, thank you.'

She hadn't realised Quinn was right behind her and bumped into him when she turned around. He showed no sign of moving. She could only get past him by brushing up against him—something which no doubt would give Quinn great amusement. 'Excuse me, please...'

She didn't want this; she didn't want to feel Quinn's heat warming her, or the power in his body reminding her of what they'd shared. She certainly didn't want him towering over her, or his hard, muscular frame awakening memories better left undisturbed.

She exhaled with relief when Quinn stood back. 'I would prefer it if we could keep everything between us on a professional level,' she said, staring into eyes that were nowhere near convinced.

'Suits me.' A faint smile played around the corner of Quinn's mouth.

'We'll have the presentation ready for you very soon. My girls are ready.'

'And you, Magenta?'

'I'm ready too,' she assured him.

The crease in Quinn's cheek deepened. 'Any chance you might have lightened up by the time the party comes around?'

'I'll be on the cocktail bar,' she said. 'And I'll mix you anything you like.'

Quinn hummed. 'I take it you have something appropriate to wear?'

'An apron?'

'I was thinking of something a touch more glamorous than that.'

'Something you'd approve of?'

'Pleasing me would be a first.'

Short memory, she thought. 'I won't be trying to please anyone—I'll be wearing one of the products your team is eager to push in the campaign.'

'Now you've got me worried. Are you going to give me a clue?'

'Paper?' She kept her face admirably straight.

'Paper?' Quinn frowned, but then his eyes began to dance with laughter. 'You're going to wear a paper dress?'

'Apparently they're going to be the next big thing.'

'Is that right?' Quinn said. He even held the door for her, and was still smiling when she left the room.

The day of the presentation dawned bright and clear. Quinn kept everything close to his chest. He hadn't been in the previous day, and Magenta had missed the electricity between them as well as Quinn's ironic glances and challenging stares. The office had ticked over while Quinn had been away, but had lacked some essential spark. Now he was back.

Magenta's heart rate soared when Quinn strode into the office, and she wasn't the only one to be affected. He had changed the mood in an instant from diligent to enthused— and no wonder; Quinn looked like a film star with his tan, his build and bearing.

Magenta was pleased she had gone the extra mile with her appearance for the all-important meeting. Jackie Kennedy had set the pace for the elegant woman of the sixties, with the clean lines of her Oleg Cassini fashions, and this morning Magenta was wearing a copy of one of the beautifully tailored suits the girls were keen to feature in the ad campaign. A better bet than paper, Magenta thought wryly. The men didn't stand a chance if they were pushing things like that. She had made sure the girls had the first choice from the rail of stylish garments which the photographer had left in the staff room, but she couldn't have been more delighted with the soft red suit Nancy had kept to one side for her.

'Nice,' Quinn said briefly, looking Magenta up and down. 'Call everyone in, will you?'

Would he ever change?

Never, Magenta concluded.

Would he ever pause to take breath? Rarely, she thought, remembering the non-stop action in his bed—which was the only encouragement her cheeks needed to fire up to the same shade as her jacket.

Oh yes, it was a triumph, Magenta agreed with the other girls later. Quinn had chosen their ideas hands down. 'But no crowing,' she insisted. 'Especially not if there's someone in the office you like. Remember, no man likes to be put down.'

'Like we've been for years?' Nancy countered, still glowing from her promotion to assistant account-executive.

'Men are more fragile,' Magenta said thoughtfully. 'We have to protect their egos if we want the best out of them.'

'Just as they have to treat us as equals if they want the best out of us,' Nancy put in.

'You're right,' Magenta agreed. 'Respect has to be earned on both sides.'

'And you have to lighten up.'

Magenta huffed wryly at Nancy's comment. 'Someone else said that.'

'Let me guess…' Nancy murmured, sucking her cheek.

'Never mind who said it. We're fighting for equality, and that's a serious business.'

'So is partying,' Nancy insisted. 'So we're going to put our concerns about the men's ability to contribute anything remotely useful to an ad campaign to one side for now and give them chance to schmooze us. But if we're going to party you have to, too. And you have to be nice to Quinn, Magenta.

He's given us this chance, so now you have to give him a chance.'

Now everyone started teasing her. 'All right, I give in!' she exclaimed. 'I will give him a chance—a tiny, miniscule chance.'

'Yeah, right,' Nancy said to a chorus of disbelieving jeers.

CHAPTER FIFTEEN

THE night of the party turned out better than Magenta had dared to expect. Her colleagues forgot their differences and started to mingle and get to know each other. Friendships were forged across the sexes, which was exactly what she had hoped would happen—and some of those friendships were heating up, which couldn't hurt. But when Quinn called her into his office she soon realised that not everything was going to plan.

She should have thought this through, she realised as Quinn gave her outfit a scorching review. 'That dress is shapeless.'

And thin. And she was only wearing paper knickers beneath her paper dress, while Quinn—alarmingly, surprisingly, incredibly—was dressed exactly as she would expect a sexy guy to dress for an evening out in the twenty-first century. He wore a crisp, white shirt with the sleeves rolled back to reveal his muscular, hair-shaded forearms, sharp jeans with an understated belt and the cleanest black shoes Magenta had ever seen. This, together with the craziest-coloured socks, she noticed now as he crossed his legs at the desk to lean back and stare at her—red, fuchsia-pink and black stripes—quirky, sexy, different. 'Let me explain.'

'Please do,' Quinn invited dryly.

'It's a paper dress,' she explained, running her hands down the offending garment. 'So you can't expect it to be cut in a sharp design. It's meant to represent practicality.'

'Well, I doubt it will ever take off in a big way, other than into a niche market. Something as ugly as that doesn't deserve to last in the realms of fashion.'

'Thanks for the vote of confidence. It's one of the products your team was keen to promote, by the way.'

'I hadn't forgotten.'

Quinn's eyes had lit—was that humour?

'Personally, I agree with you. I don't think paper fashion will fly for long, however fiercely we promote it.' But, eerily, Quinn was correct; disposable paper-garments would have a niche market in clinics, beauty salons and other places where a single wear was all that was required. Of course, she had the benefit of knowing this for sure while he could only be using his intuition. She dismissed the shiver down her spine. Quinn couldn't be aware of the future. 'At least I'm there with the theme,' she said, eager to distract herself from questions with no answers as she looked him up and down.

'As am I,' Quinn said, standing up. 'I'm guessing this is exactly what I'd be wearing if we were living in the twenty-first century.'

Magenta paled. The shiver was back again. Why had he chosen the twenty-first century in particular?

'You've done well,' he observed, lifting the slats of the blind covering his window. 'Everyone appears to be enjoying themselves.'

'I'm glad you're pleased.'

Quinn's appreciative glance sent heat dancing through her.

'You look hot, Magenta.'

'Do I?' Magenta's hand flew to her brow. 'Perhaps a glass of water…'

'Or a jug full?'

She shrieked with shock as Quinn slowly poured the jug of water on his desk slowly down the front of her dress.

'I can't believe you did that!' she exclaimed. 'You've—'

'Ruined your dress?' Quinn hummed. 'You know, I think you're right; this will never catch on.' Taking hold of the front of it, he peeled it off her.

She was shivering with a combination of shock, anger and arousal as Quinn continued his unrelenting survey. 'Stop that,' she said. 'You can't just—'

'Trial a product?' he suggested.

'I am not a product.'

'If you were, I'd buy you.'

'Like you'd get the chance,' she huffed, but fighting off images of Quinn in his role of sexual master of the universe with a shopping list in hand wasn't quite so easy. 'And what am I supposed to do now?' Crossing her hands and arms over her sodden paper-bra and pants, she glowered at him. 'Should I staple a few sheets of A4 together and go as a galleon?'

'Lucky for you, I bought a dress.'

'You bought a dress?' she queried. 'Good for you. I'm sure you'll look very nice in it.'

'For you, idiot.'

And now she *was* shocked. 'What type of dress?' she demanded suspiciously. 'I'd better warn you now, I don't do caftans.'

'Or micro-minis, apparently.' Quinn stared at her legs, where to Magenta's horror she realised her hold-up stockings were slowly slipping down and wrinkling unattractively around her ankles.

'Shame about the underwear,' he murmured, drawing Magenta's attention back to his sexy mouth. 'I guess that's gone south too.'

She tipped her chin in the air and refused to look at him. Quinn had probably bought her a prim little school-ma'am dress, complete with a coy little Peter Pan collar, long sleeves, full skirt, and a nipped-in waist—and she'd hate it.

Or not.

She stared in surprise as Quinn produced the dress.

Now she was thrown into total confusion, because this was a dress that perfectly complemented Quinn's twenty-first-century clothes. It was a figure-flattering navy-blue column of silk cut just above the knee—but the finishing touch really floored her. 'Where on earth did you get these?' she gasped as Quinn handed her a pair of sexy black suede shoes with tell-tale red soles.

'Not only am I well prepared,' he said dryly, 'I am also way ahead of my time.'

A feeling of light-headedness passed over her. She could hear the music playing outside Quinn's office. A selection of Beatles hits was just coming to an end, and the following track was some raunchy Rolling Stones.

'You seem bewildered, Magenta,' Quinn murmured as he ran the palm of one warm hand very lightly down her naked arm. 'Why is that?'

Because she wanted Quinn, with his dangerous smile and sexy eyes, in spite of the fact that he had treated her no better than a novelty product to be tested, trialled and put aside when he grew tired of it. And because there was no longer any place for reasoned thinking.

He lifted his hand away, breaking the spell. 'I'll turn my back while you get changed, shall I?'

'Yes, you do that,' she told him.

Magenta was willing to bet she had never thrown clothes on so quickly in her life. 'It sounds noisy out there,' she said as she made the final adjustment to the tights Quinn had also thoughtfully provided, along with some underwear that proved that he had both good taste and the ability to judge her size down to the nearest millimetre. 'I think I should go and check.' She didn't wait for Quinn to answer; she knew how fast he moved.

When she returned to the main office, she saw the party had really livened up. All the desks had been pushed to one side to create a dance floor, and if dirty dancing hadn't been invented yet there were certainly some hot contenders for stealing the crown. The boys and girls in the office were definitely getting to know each other a whole lot better....

'You look like you're missing out, Magenta.'

She tensed as Quinn's shadow fell over her. 'If I were looking for a partner, you might be right.'

'I am right,' he said.

Did the music have to change that very moment from heated to cool? And did Quinn have to pull her into his arms? 'Did I say I wanted to dance?'

'You didn't say no.'

The psychedelic classic *A Whiter Shade of Pale* was hardly conducive to tension, but she held herself aloof.

'Oh good—you've relaxed,' Quinn murmured against her hair.

She knew he was teasing her; she could hear the smile in his voice. 'Do you seriously expect me to relax after everything that's happened?'

'I know a way.'

They both knew a way, but whether she was ready to play with fire again was another matter.

'Do you want to go home with me? Or would you rather live dangerously in my office?'

Quinn always got right to the point. She should say no; she should do a lot of things. But the heat rising inside her was making sensible decisions impossible. And what did she have to lose? This was a dream, wasn't it? Any self-respect she might lose in the short term would be restored the moment she shook herself awake.

She wanted more than this...

But sometimes in dreams, as in life, you had to settle for what you had, Magenta concluded as Quinn led her by the hand through the press of people. The promise implicit in his grip had quickly reduced her to liquid fire, and she could only be relieved that no one turned to look at them, though the party had reached that stage where they could have walked through it naked and no one would have noticed.

'It's a huge success,' Quinn observed, shutting his office door and leaning back against it. 'And that's all down to you.'

'Hardly.'

'What have I told you about underplaying your skills, Magenta? If you don't believe in yourself, why should I? Stop with all this negative and give me something positive.'

'Will this do?' Going for broke, she wound her arms around Quinn's neck.

'It's a start.'

She heard the door lock.

Quinn's hands quickly ignited an inferno. The memory of pleasure mixed with the anticipation of more was an explosive recipe. It made her reckless, made her want to hurry things along.

'Hey,' Quinn murmured, taking hold of her hands when she tugged at his belt. 'Not so fast—haven't I taught you anything?'

Who was backing who towards the desk?

'Same underwear as the dress?' Quinn demanded, thrusting one hard thigh between her legs.

'If you mean that paper stuff that disintegrates at a touch, then yes.'

'Excellent. Let me know if this is going too fast for you.'

'I will.'

'You're on the pill?'

'Of course I am.' She blushed. Strange to think she'd been so intimate with Quinn and yet could feel so awkward and exposed when he asked her a perfectly reasonable, if unexpected, question.

'I only ask because I heard some clinics in this country will only prescribe the pill to married women.'

'But that's ridiculous.' *And quite possibly true.* This was the sixties, after all. And, though almost a week had passed in dream time, she was methodical about taking her pill each morning in the real world—even though there wasn't the slightest chance she would ever put it to the test.

Needless to say, she hadn't brought her pill with her on this crazy time-slip adventure, but that hardly mattered when she had probably only been asleep a couple of hours.

And that was her last rational thought before Quinn sank deep inside her. She had forgotten how good he was, and now she discovered that his desk was at the perfect height. He helped her up; she drew her knees back and he moved in close. Testing her, he found her more than ready. She climaxed immediately. But she hadn't finished with him yet. 'Fill me,' she commanded hoarsely. Nursing him, she worked her muscles. 'I want all of you.'

And that was exactly what she got, only now realising that neither of them had paused long enough to use protection.

They returned to the party together and Magenta soon forgot her moment of concern. None of this was real. It was wonderful, but it was still only a fantasy, and all she'd cared about while she was living the dream was that Quinn lost his brusque business-manner. He'd done more than that, Magenta realised when Quinn put his arm around her waist. Something had changed between them, bringing them closer.

Quinn remained at her side from that moment on, and everyone accepted them as a couple—though, in fairness, everyone had had quite a bit to drink by this time. The spacemen were barely distinguishable from the aliens, she noted with amusement as Quinn forged a passage through the heaving throng of green-smudged-silver people and silver-streaked green folk.

But at least she wasn't on her own when it came to the way she felt about Quinn. If anything, he was more outwardly affectionate in front of the other people than she was, and when the party finally drew to a close their destination was in no doubt.

They seemed to laugh all the way back to his house. Quinn drove smoothly and fast, and still found time to regale Magenta with stories of how far the party had gone in loosening everyone up. 'You're definitely in charge of office parties from here on in,' he told her. 'You have the knack of bringing people together.'

Never more so than now, she hoped when Quinn swung the car into the drive and they both climbed out.

They barely made it through the front door before they fell on each other, kissing and touching, as if tomorrow with all its uncertainties was almost upon them and the here and now was a fragile, unpredictable thing that refused to be captured or slowed down.

They made love on the hall rug, which fortunately was thick enough to cushion them, and wide enough so they didn't have to test the cold, hard marble floor. If there was anything nicer than snuggling up to Quinn, she had yet to discover it. When they were both briefly sated, Quinn suggested they go to bed. 'Now there's a novel idea,' she observed, laughing with happiness as he swung her into his arms.

She should have known that happiness was as fragile as time—and that it didn't do to be too greedy where either was concerned.

CHAPTER SIXTEEN

THE idyll lasted for a matter of weeks. During this time, they visited a fun fair; Quinn won a lop-eared rabbit on the shooting range and held Magenta tight when they rocketed through the candy-floss-scented air. Playing it serious, they went to an art gallery one day and to a concert the next, before Quinn changed the pace, taking her down into a cellar for some alternative musical entertainment, where the throbbing beat rang off the walls along with the sweat.

Switching styles, he escorted her to an up-town disco where they danced on a mirrored floor beneath coloured lights. On another night they saw *Breakfast at Tiffany's* at the cinema with an exquisitely beautiful Audrey Hepburn in the lead. One evening they decided to stay at home and cuddled up in front of the television, watching Goldie Hawn playing the ditsy blonde in *Rowan and Martin's Laugh-in*. Then late one night they discovered a mutual love of jazz, and ate hot dogs at a late-night cab stand after the jazz club, sharing anecdotes with friendly cabbies as they licked mustard and ketchup off each other's fingers.

She was falling in love, Magenta realised as Quinn walked her home along the embankment, where the river Thames stretched wide and silent at their side like a black-satin ribbon sprinkled with stars.

It was a wild, funny, tender, rollercoaster time, during which they grew as close as two people could grow. Now tomorrow was Christmas Eve, a time for presents, fun.and celebration.

It was definitely not a time for Magenta to be clutching the edge of the sink in the ladies' room at the office, while wondering if she was going to pass out or be sick.

I'm pregnant, she thought, staring at her green-tinged reflection in the mirror.

It had only been the one time without protection, but one time was enough. And she was sure. She had never been more certain of anything in her life—she was expecting Quinn's baby.

But how could this happen in a dream-world?

Anything could happen in a dream, Magenta reasoned, though dreams didn't usually feel as realistic as this, nor did they usually last as long. She was growing increasingly concerned—or was that hopeful?—that perhaps she really was in the sixties. There was no need for her to buy a pregnancy kit to confirm what she already knew. The changes in her body had been swift and all-consuming. She was late, sick and, more important than all of that, had the overwhelming sense that she wasn't alone in her body any longer, a fact which thrilled her beyond belief. She felt instantly protective of the tiny life inside her, even though motherhood wasn't part of her life plan, or even her dream plan. And, yes, it might have taken two to tango, but she had never asked anything of Quinn and she didn't intend to start now.

The rest of the day passed quickly, with everyone tidying up the loose ends of the campaign in preparation for the launch after the holidays. Magenta stayed behind to make sure the new top-flight team of men and women had everything they needed before she left. Quinn was still working in his office when it came time to lock up. She had some chilly hours of uncertainty ahead of her, she reflected, picking up her coat in the staff room. She was the only one who knew about her baby—Quinn's baby—and, though she could happily cope with a pregnancy, she would prefer to do so in a world she understood. 'Oh, why can't I wake up?' she murmured, without realising Nancy had joined her in the room.

'Long, hard night?' Nancy suggested with amusement. Opening her handbag, Nancy began to touch up her make-up.

'A great night,' Magenta admitted honestly. She hadn't spent a night without Quinn since the party, which was weeks ago now, and they had all been great.

'Is there something wrong?' Nancy said, turning to look at her with new interest.

'No,' Magenta said with a laugh in her voice. 'Long, hard day, that's all.'

'Are you sure that's all? You look to me like you're hiding something.'

'No, I'm not.' She was a hopeless liar. Nancy had become her best friend in this strange dream-world and Magenta was eager to share her news with someone. 'Except…I've got something amazing to tell you.'

To Magenta's dismay, Nancy paled. 'You're not pregnant, are you?'

'Why do you say that?'

'It's the first thing that popped into my mind.'

'And if I am? Would that be so terrible?' From the expression on Nancy's face, Magenta realised she was clinging by her fingertips to cloud nine—that as far as Nancy was concerned it was that bad.

'If you're married, that's fine. If you're engaged, that's almost acceptable—though it would raise eyebrows and cause a whole world of unwanted comment here.'

Magenta laughed incredulously. 'Are you saying only married women can have children?'

'That's the usual way, isn't it?'

Dumbstruck, Magenta stared at Nancy, a girl she had thought so feisty and up to the mark in everything.

'You're having Quinn's baby, right?' Nancy demanded in her usual forthright way.

She nodded.

'And you're seriously considering going ahead with the pregnancy?'

'Of course I am. What else would I do?'

'How long have I got?' Nancy murmured under her breath.

'You disapprove?' Magenta couldn't have been more surprised.

'*I* don't, but everyone else will.'

'But it's no one else's business. I'm not asking for help. I won't be a burden to anyone. I won't even expect Quinn to take an active role in bringing up his baby if he doesn't want to.'

'Boy, are you naïve.' Nancy was full of concern now. 'Honestly, Magenta, I always thought you were smart, but now I'm not so sure. Can't you see what this will do to your reputation? Oh, forget that,' Nancy said, shaking her head in exasperation. 'You won't be able to work, so what will your reputation even matter?'

'That's a little dramatic, isn't it?' Magenta demanded wryly. 'I can't see why it should change anything.'

'And how many unmarried mothers do you know?'

'Well, none in this—' She had been about to say 'this world' but quickly held her tongue.

'Do you have family who can care for the baby while you work?'

'No, but what about childcare?'

'Childcare!' Nancy exclaimed. 'What planet are you living on? And without money to support yourself you're going to be in a real bind, Magenta. You have no idea what's ahead of you, do you?' Nancy demanded, staring her in the eyes. 'If you did, you wouldn't want this baby.'

'Nancy, no, stop it. I can't believe you mean that.'

'You'll be finished in advertising,' Nancy said in a calm voice that really frightened Magenta. 'And all the men here will have a field day.'

'Then we won't tell them.'

'Not even Quinn?'

'I'll choose my time.'

Nancy laughed, but it was a hollow sound. 'Yes, you do that,' she agreed.

'And as for being finished…'

'It's not you, Magenta,' Nancy was quick to say. 'It's what everyone will think of you.'

'And what will you think of me?'

'I'm sorry you even have to ask that question,' Nancy told her, meeting Magenta's stare. 'My feelings won't change—and I'll help you all I can. You just can't expect Quinn is going to step in, or that he'll even acknowledge the baby is his. He only has your word for that. I'm sorry, Magenta, but that's the truth and I'd rather I say it than you hear it from someone else…'

Of course—no DNA tests, no proof. No help of any kind for single mothers in the sixties—that was what Nancy was telling her. How had women managed? Magenta felt as bad as she had ever felt in her life—not for herself, but for all those women who had been treated so shabbily. 'And what if I don't care what people think? What if I make a go of it?'

Nancy said nothing, which was an answer in itself.

Magenta shook her head. 'I'm not ready to have this conversation,' she admitted. 'It's too soon. I'm still getting over the thrill of discovering I'm pregnant. I hadn't thought of it as a problem, or anything remotely close. I'm sorry, Nancy, I shouldn't have burdened you with this.'

'Who else can you confide in?' Nancy pointed out with her usual pragmatism. 'Don't worry about me. It's you I'm worried about. You should take some time off work, try to come up with a plan. I'll help you.'

'I don't want to take time off work—I'm pregnant, not ill.'

'But when you start to show?'

In the sixties, that would be her cue to feel ashamed, Magenta presumed, imagining the reaction from the men in the office. But would she even be here that long, or would she wake up long before then? Uncertainty hit her like an avalanche. What could she count on in this strange, disjointed world?

Sensing her desperation, Nancy gave her a hug.

'I'm all right,' Magenta insisted, pulling herself together. She would have to be. There was some irony in the fact that she had researched most things about the sixties except for this. But, if Nancy's concern was anything to go by, impending motherhood must have been a nightmare prospect for a single woman in the sixties.

But that was no reason to give up. She had a baby to fight for now, and if people were as narrow-minded as Nancy suggested then she'd find a way to start up her own ad agency— working from home, if she had to. She would make this work and support her child whatever it took.

But then another, bigger problem hit her: would she still be pregnant in the real world? And, if the answer to that was no, did she want to wake up?

Maternal instinct was a formidable force, she realised as Nancy continued to offer advice. 'Some women have no alternative but to have an abortion or give their child away.'

'Then I feel sorry for their unimaginable plight, but I'm not one of them.' Discovering first-hand what it had been like to exist in an era where the single mother had been stigmatised made Magenta long to be able to go into battle for each and every one of them.

'And when some men find out you're pregnant,' Nancy went on, 'they'll assume you're easy meat.'

'Then they'll soon learn they're wrong. I'm sorry, Nancy—I

don't mean to have a go at you. It's just that this is all so new to me. But don't worry; I will sort it out. And I'm going make a start right now by telling Quinn.'

'Good idea,' Nancy agreed. 'You should before you pass out, or you're sick on someone's shoes.'

Magenta managed to wrestle up a smile for her friend at the door. 'I'll try not to be sick on your shoes.'

'That's all I ask,' Nancy said, playing the same game with a faint smile in return.

Quinn was packing up his things when Magenta knocked on his office door and walked in. Before she had found out about the baby, they had agreed to meet in town for something to eat, but events were moving too fast to wait for that.

'Hey,' he said, looking up. 'Hungry already?'

She stood for a moment just drinking him in. Quinn had announced that the last day before the holidays would be a dress-down day. No one did casual better than he did and, in faded jeans and a leather jacket left open over a close-fitting top, he looked amazing. But it wasn't Quinn's physical features that drew her; that was the least of it. It was the warmth in his eyes and the curve of his mouth. She wanted to frame that and remember it, as if tomorrow was coming round a lot faster than she wanted it to, and then everything would change.

'Well, come on,' he said. 'Spit it out. I know that look.' Still leaning over the desk, he gave her the Quinn smile, the one with warmth, fun and trust in it.

She took a breath and began. 'I know I told you I was on the pill.' She didn't need to say anything else. Quinn's face had already changed. Frown lines had deepened between his eyes. 'I know it was only that one time…' she went on.

'When circumstances overcame us?' Quinn straightened up.

That's one way of putting it, Magenta thought as anxiety

started to build inside her. She couldn't read Quinn. She didn't have a clue what he was thinking.

'You're pregnant?'

'Yes, I am.' They had grown so close, yet suddenly Quinn was like a stranger standing in judgement on her. 'I don't want anything from you.'

'Why not?'

That was the one question she hadn't anticipated. 'Because I can manage this on my own.'

'So, you're cutting me out?'

'I just don't want to be dependent on anyone.'

'Sounds to me like I'm going to be a father but you'd prefer I didn't interfere.'

'I'm sorry if it came out that way, it's not what I meant.'

'How do I know that?'

'You'll just have to take my word for it.'

'Like I took your word for the fact that you were on the pill?'

'Aren't we both equally responsible?' Now she was getting mad.

'Well, of course we are, Magenta, and I'm happy to accept full responsibility. I only wish you could be as straight with me.'

'I am being straight with you.'

'Are you? I feel like I don't know you—like you're hiding something.'

'I can explain.'

But she couldn't. How could she explain what she couldn't understand? How could she tell Quinn that this was a dream and that she might wake up at any moment to find out that none of it was happening?

Quinn's sound of exasperation forced her to refocus. 'Why don't you tell me what's really on your mind, Magenta?'

Quinn was waiting for answers and she had none. *This is a dream*, she wanted to blurt out. *I'm locked in a dream and*

I can't get back. 'The pregnancy was a shock to me,' was the best she could manage.

'A shock to *you*?' Quinn queried. 'This is a baby we're talking about. How can you talk about the creation of a child as a shock and expect me to be reassured?'

'Because I can handle it.'

'You can handle it,' Quinn repeated angrily. 'This is my child too, Magenta. Do you seriously expect me to take a back seat and leave every decision to you?'

She hadn't factored Quinn wanting a child into her thinking. She hadn't thought about shared responsibility at all.

'What gives you the right to do this on your own?'

She knew no other way. Since forever it had been Dad and her—the two of them. She had been raised in a single-parent family. 'I love my baby,' she said simply. 'And I never intended to hurt you.' Some things were impossible to lie about or to hide.

CHAPTER SEVENTEEN

IT WAS the first time Magenta had heard Quinn so impassioned on any subject. He would fight for his family and stand firm as a rock in the face of any difficult decision. Under any normal circumstances, that was just the kind of father she would want for her child. But she couldn't make any promises to Quinn in this strange world of imagination and dreams.

'Have you nothing to say?' he said sharply. 'Why is that, Magenta? Have you got what you came for?' he said suspiciously. 'Are you planning to leave now and take our child?'

'Please don't make this ugly Quinn.'

'It is what it is,' he rapped. 'A woman I thought I could trust—a woman I care about—cannot be honest with me. What am I supposed to think? That you're a single woman who has always longed for a child, maybe? Who knows what lengths you'd go to?'

'Don't!' Of course she had heard of men being used as sperm donors—usually with their full permission—but doing such a thing herself had never occurred to her. 'I could never be so cold-blooded.' And when Quinn made a sound of contempt, she exclaimed, 'I love you, Quinn! How is that using you?'

'You love me?'

The tone of his voice chilled her to the bone. 'Yes, I do.'

'Then your idea of love and mine are poles apart. To me, love means trust—sharing.'

'I love you and our baby.'

'Words come easily to you, Magenta.'

She exhaled in a rush, shock hitting her in the chest like a punch.

'Let me replay this for you,' Quinn said in a chillingly calm voice. 'You come into my office and announce that you're pregnant—then you barely draw breath before telling me that you don't want anything from me. How convinced would you be of my integrity if the tables were turned, Magenta? What gives you the right to make the rules?'

She didn't want to fight, but she was in no position to make promises of any kind when she inhabited a parallel universe. And, even supposing she could revisit this world in her dreams, would a hook-up on some cosmic interchange ever be enough for them? It was hardly a sound foundation for a family.

'Good to see you're ready with your answer,' Quinn snarled.

She blocked his path to the door. 'Please don't walk out on me, Quinn.'

'Don't lie to me.'

'I have never lied to you.'

'Then open up, Magenta!' Quinn roared this as he seized her arms. For a moment she thought he was going to shake her, but instead he loosened his grip and whipped his hands away, murmuring furiously, 'What's happening to me?'

You too? she felt like saying. But if Quinn was also a visitor to this strange dimension it really would be too much to take in.

Exhaling heavily, Quinn turned away, and he remained aloof from her for a long while. When he finally turned back to face her, he was calm again. 'Forgive me,' he said levelly.

'There's nothing to forgive.'

'Shock, surprise—the force of my feelings. Whatever the excuse, I shouldn't have lost it like that.'

'We're both on a steep learning-curve here.'

'And I like to think I have all things covered.'

'But not babies?' Magenta suggested softly.

'Not babies,' Quinn agreed, giving her an assessing stare. 'Are you going to be all right?'

'Of course I am. I'm going to be a mother.' She couldn't keep the joy out of her voice. Just saying the words made her feel privileged, happy—ecstatic. The difficulties could be overcome, *would* be overcome.

Sensing her inner strength and determination, Quinn shrugged. 'Looks like you've got it all in hand.'

Magenta smiled. 'There still room for a father in the picture—if he wants to be included, that is. I can understand this has come as a shock to you.'

'To put it mildly,' Quinn agreed.

'And I'm sorry if you think I've been keeping things from you.'

'Aren't women supposed to be enigmas?'

'Like the sphynx?'

'Like Magenta Steele,' Quinn said, eyeing her keenly. 'You're definitely a one-off.' He shook his head. 'No one could deny that.'

She smiled at him a little hesitantly. With the bounce of joy when they talked about their baby came the dread of separation. And now Quinn had just made that worse by caring so much.

'Whatever you want to do, I'll be here for you, Magenta.'

Quinn couldn't know how poignant a statement that was. *And I'll always love you*, Magenta thought, staring deep into his eyes. If she could only bind this moment and keep it just the way it was for ever.

'You're sure you want this baby?'

'Absolutely sure,' she confirmed.

'Good.' Quinn stared at her for a moment, and then he drew her close. 'Now all you have to do is tell me what you're hiding from me, Magenta.'

He knew her too well. She might have known he would ask, and what could she tell him? If she told Quinn the truth he'd think her mad—and, worse, he'd think her incapable of looking after their child. 'Can't we just have now?'

'Now?' Quinn pulled back to stare at her with eyes that were shadowed with as many secrets as her own. 'What is "now", Magenta? This breath? This day? This dream we call life?'

She could feel him pulling away from her, feel the distance growing between them as surely as if Quinn had removed his hands from her back and his breath from her face. She wished she could find the words to heal the broken bond between them, but there were no words. Now Quinn was walking away from her, closing himself off in every way there was.

But then he stopped and turned. 'We have to make this work,' he said. 'I'm not sure how we're going to do that yet, but I'll find a way.'

The breath caught in her throat. She knew she should be happy, and she would have been if she hadn't known theirs was a problem Quinn couldn't seize hold of and fix.

'Don't look at me like that,' he said, sensing her concern. 'This won't come together unless you believe in me.'

Quinn was a warrior who refused to accept defeat, and for one crazy moment it occurred to Magenta that he might be wrestling the same mysterious forces that she was. That was too much for her bruised and battered brain to take in. But he did seem to be staring past her to some place she couldn't see, and she let out a relieved breath when his storm-dark eyes focused on her face again. 'You don't have to be part of this, Quinn.'

'I'm determined to be.' A faint smile touched the corner of his mouth. 'Who'd have thought?'

Yes, who'd have thought? But she could no more plan for a future with Quinn than she could wake up. And how long could she keep up this deception? Could she lie to the father of her child? 'Quinn, there's something I must tell you.'

'Not now, Magenta. I know you're worried about the future and I can understand why. I know you want me to tell you where this will lead, but truthfully I don't know.'

How could he know when she was nothing more than a sham, an illusion, a figment of her own imagination? 'This isn't what you think.'

'You're pregnant with my baby. How different can it be?'

You have no idea, Magenta thought.

'Unless it's not my baby?'

Quinn's stare frightened her. 'Don't say that.' She couldn't bear to see the doubt in his eyes.

'Is this my baby? It's a simple question. Is the child you're carrying mine, Magenta?'

The air between them was suddenly charged with fury and passion, but she stared into Quinn's gaze without flinching. 'Yes, I'm carrying your baby. And realising that was a shock to me to begin with,' Magenta admitted. 'But now I can only think of my pregnancy as an unexpected blessing.'

Quinn stared at her in silence and then he said, 'You are the mother of my child, and as such I will always protect you.'

'I can look after myself, Quinn.'

'You won't have to. You're not alone.'

For that she was grateful. Becoming a single mother in a world she understood was one thing, but here?

'You should be smiling, Magenta.' Quinn said, sensing her doubt. 'This is a happy day, isn't it?'

'Of course.' And now she felt guilty. She didn't deserve this man, and she certainly didn't deserve the gift of a child. 'Quinn…' She didn't know where to start, but she had to tell him. She had never imagined Quinn would be so deeply loyal or so complex. She had underestimated him in so many ways, but he was right to say today was precious. She wanted nothing more than what she had here and now. Surely it was a small thing in the scale of the cosmos to be with the man she loved so they could bring up their baby together? To make a home for it surrounded by love? Knowing that it was an impossible dream was killing her.

'Why so serious?' Quinn demanded.

The last thing she wanted was to add to his suspicions by allowing a moment to pass, and then another, when she could have told him—when she *should* have told him. It was getting to the stage where she wished for his sake that she could just close her eyes and wake up in a world she could make sense of.

Misreading the signs, Quinn embraced her, and the moment when she might have told him passed. This was what she wanted more than anything—to be with Quinn—and it was the one thing she couldn't have.

She clung to him in desperation and when he released her she saw a different expression in his eyes. It was an expression she knew, an expression her body responded to immediately.

Quinn's lips curved. He was an unrepentant hunter; he was hungry and so he ate. 'You're the mother of my child.' He stared her in the eyes. 'And you just reminded me why...'

'Quinn...' She was already responding.

Quinn was aroused, hugely aroused. This was a private joke between them—that she barely had to look at him to provoke this response. She had to be careful about looking at him in public, Quinn had warned her with amusement when they'd been dancing in a club. 'Have you no shame?' she asked him now, already working on his clothes.

'None at all.'

'Just as I thought.' The ache inside her had spread like a delicious heat to encompass all her body, but Quinn shushed her and steadied her hands.

'Gently,' he said. 'I'm going to be gentle with you.'

'Because I'm pregnant?' Magenta demanded. 'Pregnant women love sex.'

'I'll bear that in mind.'

Now they were both yanking clothes off and tossing them aside. But even now there was a shadow. *Carpe diem*: seize the moment. Who knew how many they had left?

Quinn steered her back against the wall, lifting her and tugging off her underwear at the same time. She was as bad, breaking her nails on his belt in her hurry to undress him.

Locking her legs around his waist, she angled her body to make it easy for him. There was no foreplay this time, no finesse or teasing, no wasting a single precious moment.

Quinn's first thrust was enough to make her lose control, but he had taught her well, and she knew the power of delay. She held on as long as she could as he pounded her against the wall, but even as she hovered on the exquisite plateau of sensation she knew she couldn't stay there for ever. She must fall. It wasn't just the strength of the approaching climax she feared, but the feeling—the sense, the premonition—that when she fell this time it would be for good. The thought of being thrown back into a world without Quinn, without their baby, was a prospect she dreaded beyond all things. 'No, Quinn, stop,' she begged him, pressing her clenched fists against his chest.

'Am I hurting you?'

'No.'

'What, then?'

He was already moving, steadily, deeply and slowly as he stretched her, massaging her in a way she couldn't resist. 'Quinn, I can't. It's too big, too wild—too dangerous.' But as she punctuated each of these declarations with a groan of pleasure, Quinn took no notice. 'I'm locked in a dream and I don't want to lose you,' she managed to gasp out in one fleeting moment of lucidity.

'If you're locked in a dream,' Quinn said fiercely, 'then I am too.'

'No,' she begged shaking her head from side to side. 'We can't do this together.'

'Haven't I always promised to keep you safe?' Instead of slowing, Quinn adjusted his grip on her buttocks so he could take her more deeply.

The last thing she heard before she screamed out his name was Quinn's husky laugh against her neck, and then there was a fire-burst of light behind her eyes and her world was all sensation.

As the violent pleasure washed over her, she clung to Quinn as if her life depended on it. But the firmer her grasp the more illusive her hold on him became. Their reality was fading, Magenta realised in despair, and there was no way to call it back. The moment she had dreaded was here—was now. She was leaving Quinn, floating away from him, floating out of his reach…

'Quinn, save me!'

But even as she cried his name she knew he couldn't hear her.

She made one last desperate attempt to reach him, but the more she strained to stay where she was the more the yawning chasm between them grew. The last thing she saw was Quinn stretching out his hands as if he had the power to defeat time, space and dimension and could snatch her back again. But it was too late. She was already being sucked into the void from where there was no return, and as she tumbled helplessly from one world to the next she was dimly aware of Quinn calling out to her. But then even his voice lost its power to hold her and she slipped away.

CHAPTER EIGHTEEN

'DAMN the woman!' Gray Quinn's face was thunderous as he hammered on Magenta's office door with his fist. 'Magenta! Answer me! Magenta, are you in there? Are you all right?'

The silence was deafening. Straightening up, he braced his shoulder.

Within micro-seconds of him preparing to take action, the door opened and a wan face peered out.

'What the hell are you playing at?' he said, pushing past her. 'Have you been here all night?' He heard the door close behind him and wheeled around. 'You look awful. We've all been worried to death about you—me in particular.'

'Why you in particular?'

Her voice was like a feeble reed, which only added to his suspicions. 'We had a meeting at nine o' clock sharp. Remember that?'

Raking her hair, she looked at him in bemusement. 'Oh, I'm sorry,' she said as reality dawned.

'You don't show for the meeting,' he rapped out. 'And then I hear you're locked in here.'

'But Tess keeps a spare key.'

'Tess had a dental appointment this morning. So why the locked door, Magenta?'

'I felt safer.'

'Safer?'

She didn't answer. Rather than acting like the sharp

executive, with the smart line in repartee to match the sassy copy she wrote for her ad campaigns, Magenta was staring at him as if he was an apparition—as if she didn't know what day it was. Even odder to him was her bemused acceptance—he'd expected the woman he'd met and flirted with yesterday to be furious to learn the biker she'd dismissed, and possibly even flirted back with the day before, and her new boss had turned out to be one and the same. He gave the office a thorough scan. 'Have you been drinking?'

'I have not!' she exclaimed indignantly. 'I've been working.'

'Commendable.' There were no bottles, but he saw the work laid out on the desk. She had been working and now she looked ready to pass out. 'Lucky for you I have the bike here.'

'The bike...'

Her eyes slowly cleared, but she was still looking at him as if she didn't know what century it was, let alone what day. 'I'll take you home,' he explained in clear terms. 'You can shower, eat, dress and get back here with your brain in gear. Okay with you?'

'Do I have an option?' Colour was coming back into her cheeks.

'No. Just grab your coat.'

'I can't ride a bike dressed like this.' She stared down at her crumpled dress.

'Are your workout clothes still in the gym?'

'In the basement? Yes.'

'Then change into gym clothes. I'll wait.'

She started to say something, but he was already out of the door. Magenta might be a first-class creative, but if she proved to be unreliable there was no place for her in his organisation. There was just something nagging at the back of his mind that said he shouldn't let her go yet.

And if he did, Quinn reflected dryly, it would be the first time he had fired someone for working too hard.

He liked the feeling of Magenta clinging on tight with her head pressed hard against his back, but as they rode through London he could sense her tension. He was in a hurry to see her restored to her fighting best; he had no intention of buying a company and losing its chief asset in the same day, he told himself firmly as he took a short cut through the market district. It wasn't usual for him to take quite such a personal interest in his staff, but Magenta had touched something inside him. The fact that she had worked until she'd quite literally dropped played on his mind. Seeing one of the all-night open-air booths was still serving, he stopped the bike. 'Hot dog— ketchup, mustard?'

'What?' She stared at him with that same bemused expression in her eyes.

'When did you last eat? Never mind,' he said, swinging his leg over the bike. 'Stay here, or come with. Either way, I'm getting you something hot to put inside your stomach.'

She ate like a ravenous child, dripping ketchup down her fingers. She stared at the mess and frowned—it took her back to childhood, maybe. He grabbed a hank of paper tissues and wiped her hands. 'Better?' Dipping his head, he stared into troubled eyes.

She had enough smarts to refocus fast. 'I haven't made the best of starts, have I?' she suggested wryly.

'Drink your tea.'

She did so, blowing on it with attractive full, red lips before gulping it down with relish. 'Sorry. I hadn't realised how hungry I was.'

His lips curved. When he was heavily into a project, eating was the last thing on his mind. 'Work will do that to you.'

'So you're the same?' she guessed.

Her eyes were a clear, deep blue and she was staring at him keenly. 'I'm a little obsessive,' he admitted. 'Come on—let's get you home.'

He got another jolt when he walked into Magenta's house to find it furnished like a sixties stage-set. 'Nice place you have here…' He recognised an Eero Aarnio Bubble Chair, and an iconic Egg Pod swinging seat with a blood-red lining. Did she always live like this, in a fantasy world that mirrored each new campaign she was working on? He hoped not. He'd seen the notes on his desk regarding Magenta's next big campaign. It featured a safari theme. There was hardly room to swing a small cat in here, let alone a big one.

His mood changed, darkened. Was business Magenta's life? Was that all there was? A sense of isolation overwhelmed him—a sense of *déjà vu*. He had thought of little else apart from work on his drive to the top. They weren't so different.

'Is this the kitchen?' He pressed open a door. 'You go and change while I make some coffee. Do you want something more to eat?'

'No!' She laughed.

He was pleased to see it.

'You?' she said.

He felt a jolt when their eyes met. 'Maybe…' He was hungry.

'There are eggs in the fridge.'

'That's good for me. Go.'

He got busy in her neat, attractive kitchen, finding the eggs, a bowl, some cheese and plenty of seasoning. He thought about Magenta as he whisked the eggs. She concerned him on several levels. Her friend Tess had been at pains to tell him how hard she worked. She'd been holding everything together single-handed for months now, apparently, fending off her father's creditors whilst still managing to energise her team and come up with a host of brilliant ideas. She'd drawn him in.

'You're back,' he said, feeling a bolt of something warm and steady when she walked into the room. She was slender but womanly, tall, but not too tall. She was beautiful, quirky and under-appreciated—at least by a man. It was strange where his senses took him—sixth sense, his mother had called it. 'Omelette good for you?' he said on a lighter note.

'You are joking?' she protested with a laugh.

'Well, I've made an extra one. You should eat more.'

'I have eaten.' She held up her squeaky-clean hands to remind him.

'Eat,' he said, taking in the dark circles beneath her eyes.

She perched at the breakfast bar, crossing her silk-clad legs one over the other—slender legs, sexy heels, sheer stockings. He could see the outline of her suspender button beneath the fine wool skirt. 'So you're not coming back with me?' he enquired.

'I've called a cab. I hope you're not offended. It's just that it's hard to arrive on a motorcycle ready for a meeting—apart from the fact that bike-riding sends my heart-rate soaring, I didn't want to be late this time.'

She smiled faintly and he smiled too. 'Good thinking. You should look after yourself better, Magenta,' he said, noticing how in spite of all her protests she was wolfing down the omelette.

'Are you like this with all your employees, Quinn?'

'If you mean do I cook for them? No. Do I want them in peak condition producing their best work for me? That would be yes.'

'And that will be my taxi,' she said, forking up the last mouthful on her plate as the door-bell rang. 'And that was a delicious omelette. Thank you, Quinn.'

'See you back at the office.'

'You can count on it,' she said.

* * *

Magenta Steele was the consummate professional as well as a good-looking woman—though she was elusive, Quinn thought as he brought their meeting to a close. He could pin her down in business—having heard her pitch, he could be fairly certain they'd win an industry award for her sixties campaign, for example—but when it came to knowing what made Magenta the woman tick, that was a whole different ball-game.

'Dinner tonight,' he said as she packed up her briefcase. 'That wasn't a question, Magenta,' he added when she looked at him with surprise. 'If we're going to take this company where it needs to go, you and I have to embark on a crash course of familiarisation so we can do more than work together. We have to be able to read each other's minds.'

'Talking of which,' she said, a faint smile creeping onto her lips as she busied herself sorting documents, 'is the theme I suggested for the party okay with you—or do you think it too predictable?'

'Sixties?'

'Medallions, flares and lots of chest hair?' She looked at him now, looked him long, hard and straight in the eyes.

'I think I can come up with something.'

'I'm sure you can.'

But it wouldn't wait until the party, Quinn thought as Magenta left the room.

'You're impossible,' Tess told Magenta when she heard Magenta had booked a table for supper with Quinn for six o' clock that evening. 'What sort of dating time is that? And why a steak house? Haven't you heard of sexy venues and subdued lighting?'

'Not when I'm holding a business meeting—this isn't a date. Quinn and I have important things to discuss.'

'Like what? Your place or mine?'

'Like where we're going with the business. I'm only pleased that he's involving me.'

'Magenta, are you blind? First off, you're the heart of Steele Design—you're the major reason people come to us for ideas. Quinn is never going to get rid of you. And, secondly, perhaps most important of all, Quinn is one hot-looking man.'

'And my employer. I never mix business with pleasure.'

'Never say never—and by the way, you with serious frown lines sprouting like weeds on your face, you're coming with me.'

Shaking her head in bemusement, Magenta allowed Tess to drag her out of the office. It was their lunch hour and she had been neglecting her friends recently. *Calm down—go with the flow for once*, she told herself firmly.

'A hairdresser's?' Magenta said, gazing up at what seemed to be a vaguely familiar door.

'Bed-head to beauty queen,' Tess promised, chivvying her inside. 'I bring you my friend,' she told the young man with floppy hair. 'You'd better look after her, Justin. I hold you personally responsible for the safe return of this woman. She must look refreshed and years younger by the time you've finished with her—like she's never done a day's work in her life.'

'Miracles take a little longer,' Justin opined, studying Magenta critically.

'If I'm a lost cause…' Magenta was already leaving.

'Lost, you may be,' Justin declaimed in stentorian tones. 'But now I have found you all will be well again.'

'Oh, well, that's okay then,' Magenta said uncertainly, noticing Tess was blocking her only escape route to the door.

'And see she gets her nails done, will you?' Tess added in an aside. 'Something Jackie Kennedy—French manicure, perhaps? She might look like she works down a coal mine, but she's actually a creative.'

'I know the type,' Justin assured her in a theatrical whisper.

'Just make sure she's ready to play her role in a very

important sixties party tomorrow night. Oh, and she's got a date tonight, so make it sexy.'

'Got it.'

'You've gone too far this time,' Magenta complained, but Tess was already pulling faces at her from the wrong side of the door.

Magenta caught sight of her reflection in one of the many mirrors on the way out of the salon. Justin had given her a new look all right. Her hair was long, sleek and shiny, as opposed to the notorious bed-head frizz-top, as diagnosed by Tess.

Trust a friend to tell you the truth, Magenta thought wryly, brushing her long fringe out of her eyes. Justin had modelled her on one of his favourite sixties icons, he had explained, a model called Jean Shrimpton who had already appeared on the cover of *Vogue* at the age of eighteen. 'But I'm twenty-eight,' Magenta had protested.

'And don't look a day over forty,' Justin had told her reassuringly. 'That's how you will continue to look unless you allow me to work a little magic.'

It was when Justin talked about magic that the dream started coming back to her—bits and pieces to begin with, and then rushing in on her like a tidal wave she couldn't escape. Not that it had anything to do with real magic; she knew that. Dreams were the work of an over-active mind. All she had to do was slow down a bit and she'd sleep soundly at night again.

Slowing down meant walking through the park instead of powering along the pavements, but slowing down allowed more thoughts to crowd in. There had been a pregnancy, she remembered—yes, a pregnancy in a dream, but the baby had seemed very real to her. It still did…

Silent tears crept down her icy cheeks.

She wanted a baby.

Having a baby had never crossed her mind before. She

hadn't realised there was anything missing in her life. She hadn't had time to realise anything was missing; work took up every minute. Slowing to a halt in front of a park bench, she sank down onto the cold wooden slats. Stretching out her legs in front of her, she gazed across the placid surface of the boating lake. She'd made a baby with Quinn? Well, that should have brought a smile to her face.

It didn't.

Picking up a pebble, she stood up and skimmed it across the surface of the lake. Ripples spread outwards, unstoppable ripples. There was nothing she could do to change the direction of those ripples any more than she could change the direction of her life to match the dream.

There was no baby.

Wrapping her arms around her empty belly, she mourned the dream-child in wistful silence until a spike of cold wind reminded her she should be getting back. She turned reluctantly. Dreams, Magenta reflected as she hurried back to the office—who knew what secret lives people lived in their dreams?

Sometimes dreams weren't just longings, they were premonitions.

And that was crazy thinking. She shouldn't be greedy. She should think about all the things she had instead and be grateful. Wasn't that enough for her?

A hollow *no*...

Magenta had almost walked past the store when she stopped dead and retraced her footsteps. She stood in front of the window staring at the dress in silence. It couldn't be. But it was. It was the same dress—the identical dress. It was the flattering navy-blue shift dress Quinn had bought for her in the dream. She stared at it, hesitating until her heart rate reached danger point, and then she hurried towards the entrance. She had to have it...

They'd sold out of her size.

It wasn't meant to be, Magenta told herself sensibly as the sales assistant tried to persuade her to try on any number of alternatives. 'They're all lovely,' Magenta agreed politely. 'But not quite what I'm looking for.' *Not nearly.*

But she should make some sort of special effort tonight, make a good impression on Quinn for a change. She couldn't go out in the clothes she'd worn all day at the office, so she chose something modest with a twist. Minimal, loosely draped and delicately loose, it was a silk crêpe dress in a shade of ice-blue that brought out the colour of her eyes. Having thanked the woman for helping her choose, she made her way to the exit. She was still short of a costume for the party tomorrow night—and she didn't want to be predictable.

She was tired of predictable, Magenta mused as she hurried along the brightly lit parade of shops. Tess was right, she did take herself too seriously, and the party was everyone's chance to break out. Heading for her favourite vintage shop, she ducked inside.

Well, that was certainly something different, Magenta thought a little later, smiling triumphantly as she hugged the package containing her prize purchase close to her chest. She doubted anyone else would have thought of wearing the outfit she had chosen to a party.

CHAPTER NINETEEN

SHE arrived at the steak house exactly on time. Quinn did too, it turned out. They walked up to each other at the entrance with a laugh. 'Shall we skip the meeting?' Magenta suggested.

'Skip it why?' Quinn said as he held the door for her.

'I thought the purpose of this meeting was to help us to get to know each other better so we read each other's minds—it seems we already do.' Magenta smiled as the *maître d'* came forward to take her coat.

'You look beautiful,' Quinn murmured.

She was glad she had gone to the trouble of buying a special dress. 'And you look…' Was this appropriate chat for a business meeting? But Quinn did look incredible. With his thick, black hair as neatly groomed as it could be, and wearing a crisp white shirt, plain dark trousers with a heavy casual jacket, he looked tanned, vital, dark and amazing. She wasn't the only woman in the restaurant to notice.

He held her arm as he ushered her towards a secluded booth. 'You've loosened up, Magenta.'

'Have I?' She raised an eyebrow as Quinn handed her a menu.

'Your eyes aren't shooting daggers at me.'

'I haven't done that for some time, surely?'

'Since I scared you with the motorbike.'

'You don't scare me—it does.'

'Lucky for you, I brought the car tonight.'

Something looped inside her like a video playing a scene from a film. 'The Aston Martin DB5?'

'You saw me drive up.' Quinn's cheek creased as he grinned at her, and for a moment she was too startled to say a word.

'That's right,' she managed, telling herself the car was just some ridiculous coincidence. 'But who said you were taking me home?'

'Would a gentleman allow a lady to take a cab late at night?'

No. And if she attempted to go anywhere on her own she guessed Quinn would follow her at a discreet distance until he was sure she was safe. 'But it's early,' she pointed out, glancing at her wristwatch. 'Our meeting shouldn't take more than an hour, so I'll be quite safe going home on the bus.'

'You could,' Quinn agreed mildly, appearing to be intent on the menu. 'Steak small, medium or large? Well-cooked or bloody? Sauce, no sauce?'

'Fillet, medium, grilled, with salad, no sauce.'

'We'll take two of those,' he told the waiter. 'And some wine, beer?'

'Water—fizzy.'

'Done.'

It was all so normal suddenly between them, without a hint of mystery or magic to raise a single awkward question in her mind. She had to stop with the imagination. She wasn't at work now, thinking up some far-fetched ad campaign; she should be concentrating on the here and now and forget about what might have been in a dream.

'What's this?' Magenta said half way through her delicious, crunchy pudding of lemon-meringue pie and vanilla ice-cream when the wine waiter produced a bottle of champagne and opened it for them.

'A celebration?' Quinn suggested dryly. 'My guess is you've been too busy working even to think about celebrating the fact that Steele Design has a new lease of life—largely thanks to your efforts.'

'And your money,' she pointed out.

'I hope I have some skills to bring to bear too.'

'That's why I went after you.' Magenta blushed as she had a flashback to her dream. She pushed it aside. They were professionals; of course he meant business skills.

'Are you saying there's a possibility we might make a good team?' Quinn's lips pressed down attractively.

'Why not?' She held his gaze as the waiter served their champagne.

'To the future of Steele Design,' Quinn said, raising his glass.

'I'll drink to that.'

'I'll handle the business side of things, keep all the aggravation out of your hair, while you handle the ideas.'

'Sounds like a dream team to me.'

Realising what she had said, Magenta froze. She felt like a computer stalling when it couldn't handle an input overload, but Quinn didn't miss a beat. 'To the dream team,' he said mildly, chinking glasses with her.

She didn't fight him when Quinn suggested taking her home in his car. It was even colder when they got outside, and there were little flurries of snow in the air. Quinn settled her inside the strangely familiar interior and even helped her to secure her seat belt when he got in. That felt good: twenty-first-century man with old-world manners. It didn't come much better, in fact.

They continued to talk about the business, but there was always something left unsaid between them, Magenta felt, so she said it. 'Quinn, do you dream?'

'Doesn't everyone?' He turned right onto the main road, confidently negotiating the steady buzz of traffic.

'I'm talking about the dreams we have when we're asleep. I know everyone dreams during the day, but you're in control of that.' Quinn glanced at her and she could see she'd got his attention. 'You only have to think of something you want, if you want to dream when you're awake, and before you know it you're weaving a whole fantastic drama round it.'

'Is that right?' Quinn said dryly.

'You know it is,' she said, feeling a throb of warmth as their eyes met briefly. 'What I'm talking about are dreams beyond our control, like the ones we have at night. Dreams that creep up on us and take everything in a new direction—a direction we could never have dreamed of.' She laughed. 'If that makes sense?'

'It makes perfect sense to me.'

Was Quinn teasing her? It was impossible to tell. 'Do you have dreams like that, Quinn? Dreams that make a weird kind of sense even though you know they could never happen?'

'Like a parallel life that seems to be reality?' he suggested, sending a shiver down Magenta's spine. 'Sometimes.'

He drew up outside her door, leaving no more time for questions—unless she invited him inside. The light was glowing in the window. It looked welcoming, and she was glad she had left it on. Prepared for a knock-back, she decided to risk it. 'Coffee?'

Just as she expected, Quinn looked at her and shook his head. 'I only drink Blue Mountain.'

It was as if she had received an electric shock, but she controlled it. 'Lucky for you, that's the only brand I drink.' Her face relaxed into a smile. Everything warmed up inside her—or at least those parts of her that were already overheated, thanks to the Quinn effect, just heated up some more.

'Shall we?'

Quinn released her seat belt. His face was very close and his mouth was just a whisper away. How she wanted him. He could just turn and kiss her—brush her lips…

She'd settle for that, Magenta told herself, only to see Quinn curb a grin. 'You think I'm funny?'

'I think you mentioned coffee.'

'I did,' she agreed.

Coming round to her side of the car, Quinn opened the door for her and helped her out.

I could get used to this, Magenta thought. *This too*, she realised as Quinn put his arm around her shoulders and drew her close to keep her warm.

'Let me,' he said when she took out her key.

He opened the door, stood back to allow her to precede him and then followed, shutting the door behind them.

This wasn't supposed to happen, Magenta thought as Quinn shucked her coat off in one sweeping move. She wasn't supposed to tear his jacket from his shoulders and rip at his shirt buttons like a loved-crazed hussy. And Quinn wasn't supposed to kiss her as if they'd known each other longer than for ever and had been apart for far too long. They grappled with each other as if no amount of kissing or embracing would ever be enough for them and as if any future parting, however short that parting might be, was unthinkable.

'Bed,' she managed to gasp, glancing up the stairs.

'We'll never make it.'

Fighting with Quinn's belt buckle, she was tempted to agree. She'd taken quite a journey in that dream from sexual *ingénue* to sensualist, and she wouldn't be denied now.

Finally, she managed to wrest the belt from Quinn's belt loops and tossed it aside. He kissed her again tenderly, cupping her face in his hands in a way that brought the dreams back full force. She always felt so cherished when Quinn kissed her this way.

But Quinn had never kissed her before—not even close.

So why this heat, this passion? Why was this so familiar?

Then hunger overcame them and she didn't want to work it out. Their clothes lay scattered on the floor, and they found a new use for the stairs: pressing her down on one step, Quinn moved over her.

Adding to her almost unbearable arousal, she now discovered she could see everything they were doing in the hall mirror. Quinn, muscular, male and completely naked without a single imperfection—and Magenta Steele with plenty, but Quinn didn't seem to notice. He was staring deep into her eyes, showing her things that went back a lot longer than a dream.

But right now it was the present that mattered. She had seen the heat in Quinn's eyes and now his hand had found her.

'Tell me what you want, Magenta.'

'All of you.'

'Like this?'

'Yes,' she gasped as Quinn sank deep inside her. *Yes and yes again.* Nothing in the dream had been half as good as this. Lying back against the thickly carpeted staircase, she dug her fingers into his buttocks, driving him hard, while Quinn thrust deeply into her to a rhythm that was both exciting and new, yet wholly familiar.

Release was violent and simultaneous. Quinn roared something hoarsely as Magenta cried out his name. Their grip on each other was ferocious as they bucked and moaned in a paroxysm of pleasure, and when Quinn finally loosened his grip on her she lay against his chest, panting helplessly.

'Was that good for you?' he murmured dryly.

From somewhere she managed to find the strength to ball up one hand into a fist and tap it weakly against his chest.

'I take it that's a yes?'

Raising her head, Magenta stared into Quinn's eyes. Her own eyes would barely focus, but she managed a single word.

'More?' Quinn echoed. 'Bed this time, I think.' Swinging her into his arms, he took the stairs two at a time.

'Front room—big bed—'

Quinn was inside her before her head touched the pillow. It felt so right, so good; rather than abating, her hunger had grown. 'The more you make love to me, the more I want you.' This revelation was no more than the truth. Gripping Quinn's shoulders, she urged him on while Quinn worked steadily and confidently towards the inevitable conclusion.

'My turn,' she told him while she was still gasping for breath.

'Greedy.'

'Who made me that way?' Tracing the line of Quinn's sexy mouth with her fingertip, she straddled him and, taking him deep, she rocked while Quinn worked magic with his hands.

They made love through the night, with no time to dream. Quinn had the energy of a Titan, and, starved of love for so long, she matched him every step of the way. They finally fell asleep in a tangle of exhausted limbs.

When dawn woke them, Magenta's first thought was Quinn. She slumped back on the pillow with relief to find him watching her. This was definitely better than a dream.

And things got better still when Quinn was in no hurry to get away—he didn't mention work once.

'I didn't want to wake you,' he said, stroking her hair. 'You looked so peaceful. Were you dreaming?'

Their faces were close enough on the pillows for Magenta to see the slightest flicker of thought cross Quinn's eyes. 'I didn't need to.' Turning her head, she kissed his hand as he caressed her. 'Did you?'

'I can't remember sleeping so well for quite some time.'

Now she was in his arms again and any discussion about Quinn's dreams would have to wait.

'You look perky,' Tess commented when Magenta arrived in the office on the day of the party.

So much for trying to hide things from your best friend,

Magenta thought wryly as Tess narrowed her eyes to scan her face. 'Good sex? No—don't tell me. I might have to hate you.'

'We could never hate each other, Tess.'

'You're definitely pushing it,' Tess warned. 'Do I take it things are going well for you and the Mighty Quinn?'

'You know I never discuss my private life.'

'Only because you don't have one—or didn't used to,' Tess amended, glancing towards the window where they could see Quinn telling the DJ where to set up.

'Don't you think we should concentrate on getting the right mix for the fruit punch rather than the wrong end of the stick? We don't want everyone falling over after the first drink.'

'Why not?' Tess demanded. 'Last man standing's mine.'

The sixties-style gym suit, which was the outfit Magenta had chosen to wear for the party, was like a navy-blue shirt and bloomers all in one. There was a neat little collar, a breast pocket, buttons down the front and a coloured belt. Highly flattering, it was not.

What had she been thinking? Magenta wondered, turning to look at her rear view in the rest-room mirror. No need to ask if her bum looked big in this—it did. And, having seen what some of the other girls were wearing, she could only imagine Quinn's reaction when he compared her to the young girls in their tight-fitting hot-pants and micro-minis. But she'd bought the kit and now she'd play the game.

She'd been a little late getting ready, as they'd just learned Steele Design had won a major contract to promote a new colour magazine for a national newspaper, so the party was already underway by the time she was ready to join in. She refused to think of the coveted contract as a coincidence. Had she been asked to promote Shiver Shiver Pink lipstick or *Almost* underwear? No.

Magenta gasped as some new arrivals, girls she knew, ran

past her straight off the street complaining about *shivering* without their thermal *underwear*.

Was that a coincidence? Was she going to see a twist of fate behind every door?

'Oh, hi, Quinn.'

'Hi, yourself,' he said, grinning down at her as he held the door. 'You look… For once I'm lost for words,' Quinn admitted, scanning Magenta's fancy-dress outfit with a bemused expression on his face.

'You don't like it?'

'Is that what you're planning to wear for the party?'

'Well, these aren't my new work clothes, if that's what you mean.' She could have predicted Quinn's outfit right down to the red, fuchsia-pink and black-striped socks—and rather wished she couldn't. It made her head reel. 'You don't think this outfit is right, do you?'

'I think you look cute—but maybe cute is wrong tonight? You just landed the biggest contract in Steele Design's history, so maybe elegant-sexy would be better. You can still be cute,' Quinn added hastily, tongue firmly lodged in his cheek.

'That's good to know,' Magenta said dryly. 'I'll go and change.'

'But first.' Drawing her into the shadows, Quinn teased her lips apart and then he kissed her.

Each time Quinn drew her into his arms and she inhaled, touched, experienced him, it was like the first time all over again—and the first time had been more than magic. 'Hmm. I don't feel quite so bad now,' Magenta admitted when Quinn finally released her.

'And you're going to feel even better when you see what I've got for you.'

'Quinn!' Magenta exclaimed, pressing her hand to her chest in pretended outrage.

'A small gift.'

'Small? If it's something small, I can relax.'

'You can,' Quinn confirmed, drawing her with him into his office. 'Well? What do you think?' he said, standing back.

Magenta stared at the dress hanging on a padded hanger from a hook. She had to say something. It was expected of her. Good manners demanded she *must* say something. 'Thank you,' she stuttered, wondering if the world and everyone in it had gone mad.

'There's a pair of shoes I thought you might like too—and some opaque-black tights to finish off the outfit.'

She was the one who was about to be finished off, as her heart banged wildly in her chest. Did she believe in second sight? No. Could dreams predict the future? No again. So, how to explain the figure-flattering dress in navy-blue silk and the pair of red-soled shoes? 'Quinn, these are fabulous— and exactly what I would have chosen myself.' *Given a huge hike in salary*, Magenta thought, giving herself a moment to salivate over the fabulous shoes. 'How did you know what I'd like?'

'An informed guess,' he explained, thumbing his stubble.

But there was something else, something she couldn't read behind Quinn's steady gaze. 'And you're sure you don't dream at night?' she said.

CHAPTER TWENTY

THEY were both lost in their own thoughts on the drive home from the office. The party had been a huge success, with no time for further revelations from Quinn or opportunity for Magenta to dig for clues.

Which was probably just as well, Magenta reflected as she stroked the delicate panels of her new silk dress. Tonight belonged to their colleagues, and their cheers still rang in her ears. She would never have been able to join in the celebrations if she and Quinn had got any deeper into a discussion about dreams. But there was nothing to stop her doing a little probing now. 'What made you buy the dress for me?'

He glanced across. 'Intuition told me it might come in useful.'

And, as his lips curved in a grin, she pressed, 'Intuition? Do you often get presentiments about the future?'

'I get hunches,' he admitted. 'Am I psychic? I wouldn't have taken so long to get where I am today if I were.'

'Thirty-two *is* rather ancient,' Magenta agreed wryly.

'Your place or mine?'

A bolt of arousal hit her. Quinn as always had come right to the point. Reluctantly, she put her sensible head on. 'Wherever we can talk.' Quinn wasn't getting off the hook so easily this time.

'Mine's closer.'

'Sounds good to me.'

This time when they went inside she made the coffee and laid her cards out on the table right away. 'Quinn—discussion first.'

'Hmm, this sounds serious.' He reached past her for the mugs and, while her guard was down, he swung his arm around her waist. 'I'll issue any timetables we have around here.' Quinn stared her in the eyes, leaving Magenta in no doubt as to his agenda.

The click of the coffee machine was Quinn's cue to release her. 'Boy, do I need this,' he said, pouring them both a generous slug.

While he was distracted she led the way into his orangerie where they could see the stars as they talked. She trembled with awareness when Quinn came up behind her. She put her hands over his and rested back against his chest as she gazed up at the waxing moon. 'So, Quinn, do you dream?'

Quinn took the coffee mug out of her hands and put it on a small glass-topped table. 'Maybe,' he admitted. 'I'm usually asleep, so I can't be sure.'

'Quinn.' She turned to face him. 'I'm being serious.'

'Oh, really?' His faint smile was softly mocking. 'How can that be, when all you want is for me to admit that we meet up in our dreams? Crazy woman,' he murmured, drawing her close.

Quinn's eyes were warm and amused and his lips were close. It would be the easiest thing in the world to sink into his embrace and to forget about everything, but she was determined to discover the truth. 'I'm not asking you to believe in magic—and, I can assure you, I'm not crazy.'

Quinn held his gaze. 'What do you want me to say, Magenta?'

'I just want you to admit that there's more to life than what we can see and touch, hear and feel.'

Now he was grinning. 'Do you want me to lose my hard-ass reputation altogether?'

'I didn't think it bothered you what people thought.'

'It does if it impacts on the business.'

For a moment she had a flashback, and that flashback included a baby...

'Magenta?' Seeing the wistfulness in her face, Quinn drew her with him to a chair and sat her down on his knee. 'What's happened?' he murmured, drawing her close. 'Never mind all your questions, don't you think it's time you came clean with me?'

She rested still for a moment, knowing she had to tell him. She *had* to.

'How bad can it be?' Quinn prompted.

The dream? Apart from the baby—if it were possible to leave that aside, which it wasn't—the dream was not bad at all, especially with some careful editing.

So she told him, leaving nothing out—other than the fact that Quinn had told her that he loved her. She concentrated more on the fascinating detail of the sixties, including Quinn's appalling behaviour at the start.

'But you won me round in the end, apparently,' he said wryly.

'I tamed you and trained you.'

'Proves it was a dream.'

'You're impossible.'

'You're repeating yourself.'

Now *she* was smiling. Quinn's humour did it for her every time. Plus, he was intuitive and compassionate—not forgetting hot. She still shook her head at him as if he were an impossible case, before going on to recount all the incredible events from the dream. But when she came to the part about the baby she couldn't go on.

'There's no need to put yourself through this, Magenta. You want a baby—that's not so unusual.'

'But it felt so real.' She dashed tears from her eyes. 'And now I feel like I've lost it.'

'That's an anxiety dream,' Quinn told her, bringing her close to drop a kiss on the top of her head. 'You haven't lost your baby, because you haven't been pregnant—not yet.'

'Not yet?' Magenta shook her head at Quinn. 'You are definitely impossible.'

Quinn's answer was to throw her a sexy smile. 'Who knows what the future holds?'

She tried to pull away. The pang of loss and longing was still too strong to make a joke of it.

'Don't stop me getting close,' Quinn said, pulling her back onto his knee again. 'Don't shut everyone out so the only way you have to experience the things you wish for is in your dreams. Don't do that, Magenta, you'll miss out on so much—too much.'

'Says the expert.'

'My hopes and dreams have all been centred around the business—who knows what I dream about at night? I can only hope it isn't balance sheets.' He grinned.

'How do you explain my dream?'

'Maybe you worry you can't have children—or maybe you think you won't meet someone you'd like to have a baby with.' Quinn's beautiful eyes narrowed consideringly. 'Whatever. It's common knowledge you have the best imagination in the business, Magenta Steele—so am I surprised you have colourful dreams?' Quinn's lips pressed down. 'What do you think?'

Magenta wrapped her arms around her waist and remained silent.

'I'm going to tell you what I think,' he said, making her look at him. 'I think we should get to know each other outside the bedroom.' That caught her attention. 'Starting tomorrow night with a proper date.'

And, when for once she didn't argue, he added, 'I know this really cool jazz club...'

* * *

Life could be even better than a dream you could manipulate, Magenta had discovered, thanks to Quinn. She had no time for daydreaming in the weeks and months that followed; he took up all her time. Winter juddered reluctantly into spring, and then another year passed. With the first warm days of that new year the bulbs began to flower, carpeting the London parks with drifts of sunny, yellow daffodils and spikes of vivid purple, white and yellow crocuses. They took time off from work—lunch hours, coffee breaks—whenever the weather permitted. Muffled up in scarves and heavy jackets, they walked hand in hand, fingers intertwined as they talked business and pleasure, finishing each other's sentences and sparking ideas off each other—whether those ideas related to some new advertising campaign, or to the colour of the sitting room in their new apartment. Magenta always won when it came to colour schemes, though she had to fight Quinn tooth and nail over business—just the way she liked it.

But today was a special day. Today was a day for skimming pebbles across a pool.

'I have something to tell you,' she said, drawing to a halt in front of a familiar bench.

Quinn grimaced. 'Just so long as it has nothing to do with a dream.'

'No, this is real enough.' Picking up the flattest stone she could find, she angled her wrist and sent it skimming across the water.

'One…two…three…four!' Quinn was behind her with his arms looped loosely around her waist, counting the times the stone flipped up in the air as it travelled over the surface of the water. His breath warmed the top of her head.

'Does that mean we're expecting quadruplets?'

'Quinn?' Magenta swung round to face him.

'How did I guess? I can't live with you every day and fill my eyes with you without noticing those secret smiles you've been smiling, and the excitement you've been trying so hard to hide. Also, since we're pretty close,' he added wryly, 'I've noticed that you're late. So, Magenta Steele, I believe you have something to tell me?'

'Gray Quinn, you're a spoiler.' Pressing her hands against his chest, she threatened to push him in the water. Quinn didn't move an inch.

'This isn't what you want?'

'Of course it is!' Magenta exclaimed as Quinn swung her round in the air. 'And you?'

'I thought loving you made my life complete—you just proved me wrong.'

'So I'm second best now?' she teased him, snuggling her head into Quinn's hard chest.

'I think my heart's big enough to hold you and a whole football team of children safe inside it. You should know by now that you're the only woman I'll ever love, Magenta. And now you're the mother of my child,' Quinn murmured, staring straight into her eyes.

'I love you, Gray Quinn.'

'I love you too—and you just reminded me why.'

'What did you say?'

'What I've been saying to you for months now: I love you.'

Grabbing hold of the edges of Quinn's jacket, she shook them imperatively. 'No, not that—I'm talking about the actual words you said, about me being the mother of your child.'

With an indulgent groan, Quinn shook his head. 'Not that dream again.'

'There are some things you can't explain,' Magenta said stubbornly.

'Such as?'

'Words I heard in the dream that you just repeated—explain that away,' she said with a dramatic flourish.

Holding her in front of him, Quinn stared down into her eyes. 'Let's put this to bed once and for all, shall we? Everyone accepts that the subconscious plays on and on while we're sleeping—all those things we can't bring ourselves to think about during the day or don't have time for. We fall asleep and they all come flooding back—whether we want them in our heads or not. And then we embroider them to suit our deepest desires—like you desiring me, for instance.'

'What?' Balling her hands into fists, Magenta pummelled Quinn's unyielding chest. 'The world doesn't revolve around you, Gray Quinn.'

'Your world does, apparently.' He had to dodge out of the way this time.

'Okay,' said Magenta, setting her jaw. 'So what about the little things—the coincidences like the dress and shoes you bought me, also in the dream? And the hot-dog stand?' she said excitedly, growing in conviction.

'If they were all in the dream, then that was exactly as you say—coincidence. The dress and shoes I gave you aren't such a mystery. The girls leave their magazines lying about all over the office and, contrary to popular opinion, men do glance at them. I guessed the featured outfit of the month would be pretty high on your wish-list.'

'And the hot-dog stand?'

'We pass it on the way to your old place.' There was a smile in Quinn's voice. 'I don't think you can read too much into that, Magenta. You were hungry, I bought you a hot dog—whoo-hoo.'

Magenta sighed. Didn't everyone want a little magic in their life? But she had Quinn. She should be satisfied, she told herself, feeling warmth consume her as she stared into his face.

'I'm sorry if I burst your bubble, baby.'

'It's not that.'

'Yes, it is. However sceptical people think they are, everyone hopes that a little magic will touch their life. There wouldn't be a game of chance or a dating site in existence otherwise—and that's only the tip of the iceberg.'

'My dream was just that, in your opinion—a projection of my deepest hopes and fears onto my sleeping mind.'

'I'm afraid so.'

'Then I think you're an unromantic killjoy, Gray Quinn.'

'Really?' Quinn murmured, not even slightly ruffled by this opinion. 'So, what do you make of this?'

'What is it?' Magenta asked, staring at the small velvet box.

'Why don't you open it and find out?'

She did as Quinn said, only to feel every bit of blood drain from her face. 'It's fabulous,' she whispered. And it truly was.

'It's no more than you deserve,' Quinn told her, removing the flawless blue-white diamond and placing it on Magenta's wedding finger. 'Think of it as a bonus for landing the magazine account. I saw it in the jeweller's window and couldn't walk past it. For some reason, it called to me.'

'And that's all it is—a bonus for my work?'

'What do you think?' Catching Magenta into his arms, Quinn held her close. 'Do you want the full-on kneeling-in-the-mud routine, or can I ask you standing up?'

'On your knees,' she commanded.

'Heartless woman.'

Heart full, she thought.

'Magenta Steele, will you make me the happiest man in the world by consenting to be my wife? What am I talking about?' Quinn said, breaking off to shake his head. 'I'm already the happiest man in the world.'

'We don't need to get married?'

'To bring up a baby in a household full of love together? No, I don't think we do.' Catching hold of Magenta's hands, Quinn held them to his warm lips for a few intense moments, and when he looked up again his eyes were dancing with the humour she loved. 'But if you want the ring…'

'Stop teasing me, Quinn,' she warned him. And, instead of telling him to get up, she knelt down too. 'I'll take you with or without the ring, as you well know.'

'And I want you whether we get married or not—and that would be for ever,' Quinn added, staring deep into Magenta's eyes. 'Not just for the duration of a dream.'

At his mercy…and in his arms?

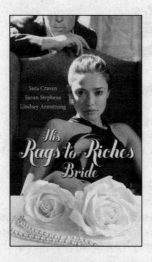

**Three glamorous and intense
Cinderella romances from your favourite
Mills & Boon® Modern™ authors**

Innocent on Her Wedding Night
by Sara Craven

Housekeeper at His Beck and Call
by Susan Stephens

The Australian's Housekeeper Bride
by Lindsay Armstrong

Available 4th February 2011

www.millsandboon.co.uk

FLORA'S DEFIANCE
by Lynne Graham

Angelo Van Zaal is convinced he should have guardianship of Flora Bennett's niece, despite Flora wanting to adopt too. There has to be a way to make Flora concede to his wishes… *and* indulge his infuriating attraction to her…

THE WEDDING CHARADE
by Melanie Milburne

Nic Sabbatini doesn't respond well to ultimatums. But when stunning Jade Sommerville announces their upcoming nuptials to the media, he may have finally met his match!

HER UNKNOWN HEIR
by Chantelle Shaw

Two years after their fling ended, Ramon Velaquez can't forget Lauren Maitland, the woman he banished. But when he finds her again, she's strong, independent, and harbouring a secret…

THE INHERITED BRIDE
By Maisey Yates

Princess Isabella didn't want to marry the Sheikh to whom she was betrothed. But after her sensual journey to the desert she was never going to be the same again…

On sale from 21st January 2011
Don't miss out!

Available at WHSmith, Tesco, ASDA, Eason and all good bookshops

www.millsandboon.co.uk

THE RELUCTANT DUKE
by Carole Mortimer

Forced to return to his family's seat, Lucan St Claire takes beautiful PA Lexie Hamilton with him. Lucan, however, has no idea that his new assistant isn't quite what she seems…

THE DEVIL WEARS KOLOVSKY
by Carol Marinelli

Swearing revenge on the Kolovskys, who abandoned him, Zakahr Belenki determines to destroy their fashion empire! Then he meets his secretary, Lavinia. Her honesty and passion for her job make Zakahr's conscience waver—and inflame his desire…

PRINCESS FROM THE PAST
by Caitlin Crews

Marriage to Prince Leo Di Marco was no fairytale, so Bethany Vassal ran away, hoping the man she loved would come and find her. Now the time has come for Leo to produce a royal heir— and Bethany must return to the castle whence she fled!

INTERVIEW WITH A PLAYBOY
by Kathryn Ross

Marco Lombardi *hates* journalists. Whisking reporter Isobel Keyes away in luxury seems like damage limitation—until she sparks his interest. Now Marco *wants* to kiss and tell…

On sale from 4th February 2011
Don't miss out!

Available at WHSmith, Tesco, ASDA, Eason and all good bookshops

www.millsandboon.co.uk

2 FREE BOOKS
AND A SURPRISE GIFT

We would like to take this opportunity to thank you for reading this Mills & Boon® book by offering you the chance to take TWO more specially selected books from the Modern™ series absolutely FREE! We're also making this offer to introduce you to the benefits of the Mills & Boon® Book Club™—

- **FREE home delivery**
- **FREE gifts and competitions**
- **FREE monthly Newsletter**
- **Exclusive Mills & Boon Book Club offers**
- **Books available before they're in the shops**

Accepting these FREE books and gift places you under no obligation to buy, you may cancel at any time, even after receiving your free books. Simply complete your details below and return the entire page to the address below. You don't even need a stamp!

YES Please send me 2 free Modern books and a surprise gift. I understand that unless you hear from me, I will receive 4 superb new books every month for just £3.30 each, postage and packing free. I am under no obligation to purchase any books and may cancel my subscription at any time. The free books and gift will be mine to keep in any case.

Ms/Mrs/Miss/Mr _____ Initials _____

Surname _____

Address _____

_____

_____ Postcode _____

E-mail _____

Send this whole page to: Mills & Boon Book Club, Free Book Offer, FREEPOST NAT 10298, Richmond, TW9 1BR

Offer valid in UK only and is not available to current Mills & Boon Book Club subscribers to this series. Overseas and Eire please write for details.. We reserve the right to refuse an application and applicants must be aged 18 years or over. Only one application per household. Terms and prices subject to change without notice. Offer expires 31st March 2011. As a result of this application, you may receive offers from Harlequin Mills & Boon and other carefully selected companies. If you would prefer not to share in this opportunity please write to The Data Manager, PO Box 676, Richmond, TW9 1WU.